Red Hot Lover

LUCY MERRITT

GW00374149

Heartline
Books

LUCY MERRITT

Lucy Merritt was born in a snowstorm and has never got over it.

She ran away from home when her ultra-green father decided the family didn't need central heating any more. Since then, she has had many jobs – from serving Sangria in a bar in Spain, to marketing fantasy hot-water bottles at Christmas.

When she fell in love with a hill farmer, she made him put a Scandinavian wood-burning stove into the marriage vows.

Lucy is adaptable. She writes in bed, solves problems in the bath and makes love in front of the fire. Everything else is negotiable.

prologue

It was a dream. Alex knew it was a dream.

She was standing in front of a flat-fronted Regency house. The flagstones were shiny from rain. It was cold and dark, but the house was lit up as if there was a spotlight on it. It was no spotlight, though. It was a huge flambeau. Naked flames beat backwards and forwards in the wind.

That's how she knew it was a dream. Houses are not lit by twelve-feet-high fire baskets in twenty-first century London.

The door to the house was open. Sounds of a party eddied out into the street. A buzz of voices. A woman's high-pitched laugh. The clink of glasses. Music. The music was the tinkly kind that did not seem to have any beginning or any end. It just plodded round like a well-tempered horse on a leading rein. It was cheery, though.

I must have seen too many Jane Austen videos, thought Alex. My dreams never used to be this authentic.

She found herself drifting inside. No feet to walk with, it seemed, though she firmed up as she went higher. Her head was positively heavy, and she could feel corkscrew curls bobbing against her cheek. Definitely too much Jane Austen.

She was facing a huge staircase, a great rococo sweep of gleaming wood, like a stole thrown round the marble-tiled entrance hall. The hall was quite empty. Nobody noticed her at all. The party was somewhere away to her right. Alex ignored it.

Without knowing how she got there, she found she was at the first landing. A tall set of double doors opened off it. Alex put a hand on the brass doorknob, but she did not have the strength to turn it. She pushed and heaved to get her real strength into her dream, but she could not. The doors stayed implacably shut.

She said, 'But I must get in.'

And the doors swung silently open.

She hesitated. She did not know what she would find in the room. The party noises were a long way away. No one would hear her if she called.

But the doors had opened for her. She could not bear to go without seeing what was inside.

It was a high room, seemingly all the taller for being empty. It was large and beautifully proportioned. It had parquet floors, an eighteenth-century chandelier and a floor-to-ceiling French mirror. She knew that room.

Oh, thought Alex, disappointed. It was only her grandmother's office. It even had Lavender's grand, Louis XVI desk, all rococo moulding and ormolu insets. Apart from that the room was empty. It should, she thought, not for the first time, have been a ballroom. Instead it was the managing director's office of Lavender Eyre and Associates. Alex constituted the Associates.

This dream was turning out to be a real letdown. She had started off going to a Regency evening party and had ended up back at work again.

One of the uncurtained windows rattled. It sounded like someone trying to break in. But when Alex went over to it – she seemed to have developed feet now that she knew she was at work – there was nothing there but rain driving against the casement.

She was not scared. She worked late too often to be scared of the big, beautiful, silent room. A bit lonely, maybe. But then party noises did that to you if you were on the outside. Even if the party was in one dimension and you were in another.

There must have been some light from somewhere because she could make out the massive, heavily carved cornice and the white walls. None of Lavender's exquisite collection of modern art had survived the transition to dreamscape. The walls were bare except for the enormous, baroque looking glass.

Maybe the light came from there. There seemed to be a gleam behind its dark surface. Curiously, Alex turned towards it. The lights seemed to curve a little as if it was beckoning. She could not see what it was reflecting. Slowly, she walked towards it.

She picked up her own image from the movement of clothes first. She was wearing something pale. It seemed to be full-length, too. And it wafted a lot. So there were draughts in this dream, just as there were in real life, thought Alex.

And then she stopped dead.

Suddenly, she was looking at herself face to face. Except that her face was only in the mirror for a split second. She caught a glimpse of features she knew all too well – eyes too dark; face too pale; nose too snub; mouth too passionate.

Someone had said that recently. 'Your mouth is too passionate, Alex. It will get you into trouble.' She desperately tried to remember who and why. She knew it was important. But, though she strained and strained, the memory danced away, continually on the edge of a name, continually dying away just as she thought she had caught it.

She was distracted. So it took her a moment to realise that her face had disappeared from the mirror. It was sudden, as if some playful giant cat had clawed her out of the way.

To make room for another face.

A man's. His eyes were as dark as hers, and he had a great hook of an Emperor's nose. He looked bad-tempered. No, thought Alex, that was the wrong word. He looked dangerous.

He looked back at her, unsmiling. Looked right into her. Alex knew he could see her, though he made no sign, any more than she did. But their eyes locked.

She knew. And so did he.

Instinctively, she looked over her shoulder. But she was still alone in the over-decorated room. The man was only in the mirror.

She had the impression that he was tall and dark-haired. But it was only an impression. There were other things about him, distinctive things that Alex knew she ought to remember. Hell, she was almost certain she even recognised them. But she could not get hold of them. They slipped away, even as she tried to tell herself to remember them and there was nothing she could do but stare into those strange intense eyes.

They seemed to be closing in on her. Or drawing her towards him. Into his world. Into him.

She thought he spoke. She thought he said, 'I've found you at last.'

She tried to back away. She tried to focus on the party noises downstairs. She tried to remember this was a dream.

It was no good.

He did not reach out of the mirror, but she could feel herself being sucked into his world. Her feet were gone, and then her shoulders. Even the curls were turning to paper, and her head was getting lighter and lighter . . .

He said, 'Come to me'. Not aloud. In her head.

It felt as if she had no choice.

She fought and fought. Her throat would not obey her. Her vocal chords would not move.

With a huge effort, Alex shouted, 'No!' at the top of her lungs.

Or she meant to shout. It came out like a mouse squeak. But it made the man in the looking glass frown. For a moment, only a moment, that terrible stare faltered.

And she was released.

It was her only chance. Alex knew it was her only chance.

She turned her back on the mirror and tore out of the room. She flung herself down the stairs. Her thistledown body had no substance now. She tumbled head over heels like a silk scarf. It did not matter. She was free.

   The party was still going on. Ignored, ignoring, she somer-saulted out of the door into the rain-drenched streets. A dark figure was approaching the house. His heels clipped on the wet flagstones. She turned to him gratefully –

   And it was the man in the mirror.

   He smiled.

   'NO!' shouted Alex.

She woke up saying it. Not shouting. Muttering hotly into her pillow. But still desperate to get away. Still feeling she couldn't.

   'No. No. No.'

   Over and over again.

chapter one

'Look. Joe, I'll be frank. You're hot right now.'

The man who had talked his way past the office assistant had teeth so perfect they could have starred in a toothpaste ad. Or served as a spare set for a shark. They were a gift to a natural cartoonist.

'Mmm?' said Joe Gomez. He was concentrating on the doodle on his sketchpad.

The man did not seem to notice that he only had half Joe's attention. He pushed a folder across the desk.

'Have a look at this. Just preliminary ideas, of course.'

It was a purple folder, bound with a gold tassel. It looked like the programme for a coronation at least, Joe thought. Oh, these English!

He did not pick it up. 'What is it?'

'Joe Gomez, the Series,' said the teeth triumphantly. 'From my perspective as a professional communicator. Of course, at this stage, it's just something to kick around.'

Joe said quite kindly, 'Sorry, I'm already committed.'

The man examined his nails. 'Ah.'

'There's going to be a follow-up to the programme you probably saw.'

'Palaces and Pigpens. Yes. My company made it.'

'What?' Joe was genuinely puzzled. 'Then why are you here? I told Tom I'd do it as long as I liked his ideas. He was still working on them the last time I talked to him.'

'And when was that?'

Joe shrugged. 'Couple of days ago, maybe. I'm not sure.'

'That would account for it. You see, Tom has moved on.'

For the first time since the man plumped himself down

unasked, he got all Joe's attention. He stopped sketching and narrowed his eyes.

'Excuse me?'

The man shifted a little, but his tone was airy when he said, 'Tom Skelton's contract ran out.'

When Joe said nothing, he added defensively, 'Television is that sort of business, you know. Producers are only as good as their last production.'

'Like architects,' said Joe grimly.

He cast a glance at the model of his prize-winning opera house on the spot-lit table in the corner. That was why The Teeth was here offering him a television series.

He said, 'I'm not hot, I'm a prize winner. And another will be along with the next prestige contest.'

'You're too modest,' said The Teeth, settling back comfortably.

So we're back on his brief now, thought Joe sardonically. He put his fingertips together and let the man pitch.

'Everyone's saying architecture is the new rock music. It's out there all the time – papers, magazines, books. The kids are interested. And you're today's man.'

'Oh?'

'Yup. Young. Fit. Enthusiastic. You know your stuff and, frankly, the chicks think you're hot. You should see the audience-response stuff we got to *Pigpens*.'

'I did.'

'Of course, you would need careful guidance, but …' The man did a double take. 'You did?'

Something told Joe it would not be a good idea to say that Tom had shown them to him.

So he ran a diversion instead, saying 'Scary! I thought viewers would talk about the buildings. But all they seemed to have noticed was my butt.'

'You got the highest approval rating I've ever seen,' agreed his visitor, enthusiastically. He whipped out a chart and passed that across the desk as well. 'Look for yourself.'

Joe flinched. 'I don't think I will, thank you.'

'Ok.' The man swung it round and read off some comments. '*Animal vitality … loved the five o' clock shadow … come-to-bed eyes …*'

'All right, all right,' said Joe. 'Does anyone actually say anything about the content? Like, does a building, any building, get a mention?'

The man pursed his lips, scanning the sheet in front of him. 'Hmmm. Buildings, buildings, building. Yes, here's one. *Looked like he could build those things as well as prance around talking about proportion. You could smell the sweat. This is great television.*' He looked up. 'How's that?'

'Not quite what I meant,' said Joe dryly.

The man leaned forward. 'Joe,' he said earnestly, 'this could be the biggest thing I've … you've … ever done.'

Joe could not resist. He shook his head gravely. 'Don't think so. Old Faithful over there,' he nodded to the Opera House, 'has got several million tonnes advantage.'

The man did not notice that he was being teased. 'Yes, but this is television,' he said reverently. 'Worldwide television.'

That startled Joe. 'Worldwide? Tom said it was just a slot for some local-interest thing.'

The Teeth flashed with annoyance, quickly curbed.

'That was before we saw the potential,' he said smoothly. 'This is nothing to do with Tom any more. We're sure you have international appeal. More important, multi-generation appeal. You look like a movie star. You're as athletic as an adventure-holiday leader. You're even self-taught.'

Joe say bolt upright. 'I am *not* self-taught,' he said furiously. 'You don't teach yourself about weights and loading and drainage. It would be dangerous. And highly irresponsible to suggest that just anyone could build something without proper discipline. I admit, I went to a lot of schools. You could say I put together my own training programme …'

The man interrupted, waving a bored hand. 'Whatever. The important thing from our point of view is that you're *accessible*. You've worked all round the world. You're a good, spontaneous raconteur. You sound North American, which is the industry norm. *And* you sweat and look great in shorts. It's perfect.'

Joe grimaced. 'That depends on your point of view.'

The man detected a joke and smiled politely. 'Now,' he said, as one getting down to business, 'We are thinking of eight programmes for the first series. Venice for the first one. Venice is very buzzy. Then the book. The video. The market is there. Believe me.'

'I do. And when does Tom get his share of it?'

'I told you. We let Tom Skelton go.'

'But it was his idea in the first place. I only did *Pigpens and Palaces* because he's a friend.'

The Teeth recomposed his features to an expression of regret. It was so false it made Joe want to hit him. He was taken aback. He had hit out a lot when he was a slum kid with an absent father and a mother who couldn't speak proper English. But that was more than thirty years ago, and he hadn't felt the urge to slug anyone since.

But this guy, with his white, smiling teeth and his two-and-a-half chins, was rapidly changing that.

Before he reverted to five-year-old pugilism, Joe said swiftly, 'It was Tom's idea. I'm not selling him out. The answer's no.'

The two-and-a-half chins came into play, suddenly very serious. A small boy playing at being a captain of industry, thought Joe. He detached himself from the argument and began to doodle again, starting with a cap and scabby knees.

'I'm talking serious investment,' the man said in hushed tones.

'I hope it works out for you,' said Joe absently, entranced with his creation.

'This could open up a whole new career for you, Joe.'

'No it couldn't.'

'I'm not joking. You could be as big as … as …' The professional communicator could not find a name. He gave up. 'Bigger.'

'Thank you for the compliment.'

The man did not recognise irony. 'I mean it.'

'So do I.' Joe finished his sketch and stood up. 'The answer's no.' He held out his hand. 'Goodbye.'

The man did not take his hand. In fact, he did not stir from his seat.

'Listen to me,' he said impressively. Well, he may have impressed himself. But the only thing he did for Joe was to make him want to pick him out of the seat and throw him out of the window.

'Listen. I've never said this before. Potentially, you've got it all.'

'Thank you. Still not interested. And I have another meeting …'

'Looks, charisma, intellect. The camera loves you. You're a natural,' said The Teeth earnestly. 'You can't lose.'

'Yes I can.' Joe gave him the sweet smile, which any one of the junior architects upstairs could have told his visitor meant that he was about to explode. 'I could lose my temper. Quite soon. Like now.'

The man stood up hastily. 'I could make you a celebrity.'

Joe laughed aloud. It had a dangerous ring.

'I don't want to be a celebrity,' he said very softly. 'I'm a working architect, not a performing flea.'

He prowled round the desk. The Teeth grabbed his briefcase, still not properly closed, and stuffed it under his arm. Papers bulged but he did not wait to return them to order. The look on Joe's face discouraged it. He retreated fast.

Joe got to the door first and opened it.

'Goodbye,' he said. 'Don't come back.'

The moment he heard the outer door close, the explosion hit.

'*Peta!*' he roared. 'Come here, you spawn of a sloth, and explain yourself.'

But the head put round the door was not the leggy receptionist's. It was one of the younger architects from the studio on the floor above. He was grinning as he held a stopwatch in his hand.

'I make that twelve minutes. You must be feeling mellow.'

Joe's maternal grandfather had been a Peruvian sea captain. He had bequeathed to his unknown grandson a mighty set of eyebrows and a stare to transfix steel. Now Joe turned his stare on the clown in the doorway.

'You opened a book on how long it would take me to kick him out?'

'Yup,' said the clown. He was Charlie, the bravest of Joe's assistants. Also the most talented, which might have accounted for his courage in the face of Joe's temper. Joe respected talent.

Joe simmered for a moment. Charlie hovered in the doorway warily, knowing it could go either way. But then Joe laughed, and he knew it was all right.

'Who won?'

'Peta, for once. Can't imagine why. The rest of us were all under five minutes. But she had twenty because she was sure you couldn't resist becoming a TV personality.' The last was not quite a question.

'I can resist,' said Joe. 'I let him stay because I wanted to find out whether a friend of mine is being shafted.'

'And is he?'

Joe smiled. It was white and predatory and, thought Charlie, rather frightening. 'Not if I can help it.'

The office knew the signs. The young architect's heart sank. 'What are you going to do about it?'

'Not sure yet.'

'I mean, you aren't going to take on any more work, are you? We're drowning upstairs. And Peta can't keep up with the admin as it is.'

Joe wandered over to his opera-house model and moved around a couple of the small people on the second level.

'She's out of her depth.' He said, almost to himself. 'They all are. What we need is a proper administrator who knows what she's doing, and can keep her head in a crisis. A diplomat with a photographic memory.'

Charlie pricked up his ears.

'Sounds like you've found someone.'

'Oh, I've found her all right,' said Joe grimly. 'The problem is convincing her that I need her, more than anyone else does. She's big on people needing her. It's her only weakness.'

'That makes a change,' murmured Charlie.

Joe looked up from the model. 'What?'

'Usually, you're their only weakness,' pointed out the other irrepressibly.

For a moment, Joe's eyes narrowed threateningly. Charlie was surprised. Lots of things roused Joe's ire. He was a passionate man, and when he was in a rage, he saw no reason to make a secret of it. But he did not usually get worked up about the women in his life. They came and went. He flirted with appreciation, and said goodbye without regret. And he was perfectly well aware that the guys in the drawing office had a bet on how long each one of them was going to last. He even told the girls themselves about it, if he really liked them. Flirt though he was, he was honest.

Charlie had never encountered that dangerous look when he had teased Joe about one of his girlfriends before. Maybe this one was important, he thought.

But then the fierce look disappeared and Joe was laughing ruefully.

'Not a chance. She's a hell of an administrator, but her taste in men is still in the Dark Ages. I don't rate. And if I did, she wouldn't look at a job here. She's professional to her toes.'

'Sounds like Heaven,' said Charlie wistfully.

They contemplated a well-run business in companionable silence for a moment.

'Any chance of getting her to join us? We're doing great. We can afford it.'

'No, money won't do it. She's loaded, unfortunately. No, I'll have to convince her she's needed.' Joe brooded. 'I'm still working on it.'

'Then we'll get her in the end,' said Charlie encouragingly.

But he went back to tell the guys that there was a new woman to bet on. And this time, it looked as if Joe Gomez was not getting it all his own way. That would make for an interesting calculation of the odds. They had no form for that one.

'Alex, what's wrong?' Julie Carter looked at her flatmate with concern.

They had been at school from the age of five. Now they were twenty-eight and best friends. Julie was an actress for whom great thing were prophesied, while Alex was, as she herself said wryly, 'the office boy in the family firm'. Julie was talented, extroverted and wildly sociable. Alex stayed home and read books, every chance she got. They had nothing in common, yet understood each other completely.

So when Julie saw Alex sitting at the breakfast bar staring into space, she knew something was wrong. Alex was not temperamental. If something upset her, she dealt with it in her quiet way. She did not droop over her barely drunk coffee as if the end of the world was coming. That was usually Julie's prerogative.

So now Julie was worried. 'You look like hell,' she said now. 'What's happened?'

Alex jumped and turned.

'Oh Jules. I didn't hear you.'

'That's because you were on Planet Disaster.' Julie hoisted

herself up onto one of the kitchen stools. 'Tell all.'

Alex shook her head.

'Come on, don't be mean. I tell you all my horrors,' wheedled Julie.

'It's not a horror. At least …'

'You've lost all your money and are going to have to scrub floors,' guessed Julie cheerfully.

Along with the administration of her grandmother's company, Alex had inherited what she admitted was a disgusting amount of money. It had bought the Regency mews house she shared with Julie. It also meant that Alex did not have to work unless she wanted to.

So far, she had always wanted to, though the last couple of years of working at Lavender Eyre's cosmetics house might just have changed her mind, thought Julie. Her grandmother was a snob and a tyrant, and Alex hated cosmetics, anyway.

'Scrubbing floors I can do,' said Alex dryly.

Julie grinned. Alex was also a lot more domestic than she was. 'Ok. Let's think.' She thought about Alex's warring family and hazarded another suggestion. 'You're running away to sea.'

'I wish.'

'You should,' agreed Julie. 'All right. You're still rich and you're still here. What else could go wrong?' She snapped her fingers. 'I know. Your grandmother has sacked you.'

Alex pulled a face. 'Some hope,' she said instinctively. And at once, 'No, I don't mean that.'

'Yes, you do. But I'm willing to forget you ever said so, as long as you tell me what's really wrong.'

Alex laughed. 'You drive a hard bargain,' she growled, quoting from their childhood detective game. Her laughter died abruptly. 'Oh Jules, I don't know what's happening to me.'

'Great,' said Julie comfortably. 'Equal at last. I never know what's happening to me. Tell all.' She hopped off the stool

'Want a beer while you talk?'

Alex shook her head. 'No. I've got to go to one of Lavender's parties in about an hour. I was sitting here trying to psych myself up for it.'

Julie was watching Alex shrewdly.

'Is that all? Cold feet?'

'You know me. I'm not good at parties.'

'You're as good as you want to be,' said Julie

It was true. Alex was one of the world's listeners. So she was always a welcome guest. In her quiet way, she had rescued many a party that was dying on its feet, including a couple of Julie's. They both knew it.

But now she was shaking her head, looking depressed.

'Not cocktail parties. I'm six inches too short. And I hate to think how many inches too wide.'

'It's the "I've-got-nothing-to-wear blues", is it?'

Alex gave a snort of laughter. 'Oh, I've got something to wear all right. Lavender just sent it over.'

'Ah.'

'Don't say "Ah" in that knowing way. Lavender's got exquisite taste.'

She sounded so depressed about it that Julie almost choked on her beer. 'What has she sent you?'

'Oh, I don't know. Something black,' said Alex without interest. 'She says I'm to wear the Egyptian earrings with it.'

'Restrained exotic,' said Julie knowledgeably. 'Good choice.'

Alex narrowed her eyes at her. 'You can go off people, you know. Whose side are you on?'

'What's wrong with looking good?' countered Julie.

'What's right with looking ridiculous?'

'Your grandmother would never send you anything that made you look ridiculous,' said Julie positively.

Alex glared at the countertop. 'Just stuff that makes me look like someone else,' she muttered.

Julie was unimpressed. 'So go mutiny! Wear something you chose yourself.'

'But that would hurt her feelings.'

'Oh, for God's sake, Alex,' said Julie in disgust. 'You can't let other people's feelings dictate your whole life.'

'I don't. Not my whole life. Clothes aren't important enough to make anyone feel bad about, though.'

'Then bite the bullet and wear the dress,' said Julie, who thought clothes were marginally more important than food or sleep.

Alex heaved a sigh. 'Yes. I know.'

Julie hitched herself back onto the barstool. 'That isn't what's really worrying you, is it? There's something else,' she said in a voice of discovery.

Alex swirled the cold coffee around in her cup. She did not answer for a moment. At last she said slowly, 'Do you ever have dreams, Jules?'

'I have nightmares about getting on stage and finding I've learned the lines for the wrong part, if that's what you mean.'

Alex smiled. 'No, not nightmares. Dreams. The sort that stay with you after you wake up. Not scary or anything. Just dreams you remember.'

Julie stopped teasing. 'I suppose everyone does sometimes. Depends how soon you wake up after, doesn't it?'

Alex watched the coffee absorbedly. 'Do you think they mean anything?'

Julie wriggled on her barstool. She was intrigued.

'What did you dream then?'

'It was a lot of nonsense.'

Julie maintained a hopeful silence.

Alex gave a little laugh and gave in. 'Running away. Nothing dramatic. Probably a classic anxiety dream.'

'Running away from whom? You weren't leaving Rupert at the altar, by any chance? I wouldn't mind that being prophetic.'

Julie did not like Alex's long-term boyfriend, and made no secret of the fact. Alex had given up being upset by it. These days, she just treated it as a joke.

'No, Rupert didn't figure at all.'

'But somebody else did,' Julie diagnosed. She thought about it and then said slowly, 'A man. Yes, of course a man.'

Alex swallowed and would not meet her eyes.

Julie was more and more intrigued. When they first started sharing the house, acting jobs had been thin on the ground. Julie had had to fight for every job. Sometimes the rejection was brutal. She had masked her insecurities by ricocheting from man to man.

But Alex never laughed or cried or sat up all night over a man herself. She went out with men, of course. But she kept the relationships strictly within the bounds of friendship.

'I'm a one-man woman,' she said once, when Julie protested about her passionless life. 'I always have been. What's the point of playing the field when I already know the man for me?'

When that man turned out to be Rupert Sweetcroft, Julie was frankly appalled.

They did not have pet names for each other. They did not share private jokes. Rupert stayed overnight sometimes, but in the morning he treated Alex with exactly the same degree of intimacy as Julie – which was to say, none at all. They did not hold hands when Julie was not looking. They did not even kiss when he left.

'So, what were you doing in this dream of yours to embarrass you?' Julie asked. 'Making mad, passionate love to the postman?'

Alex was startled into a laugh. 'No, of course not.'

'Well, who? Not Rupert, obviously.'

'No, I told you. Rupert wasn't in the dream. No one was in the dream. Well me and …' She spread her hands despairingly. 'I don't know who.'

'Sounds exciting. What was he like?'

Julie thought Alex would laugh again. But she did not. 'Come on. No need to be ashamed about not dreaming about Rupert.' She added, not very tactfully, 'No one in their right mind would dream about Rupert.'

That roused Alex. 'Oh Julie. I wish you'd be fair to Rupert. Just sometimes!'

'Fair!' Julie said, outraged. Julie was good at outrage. Full-blooded indignation had won her several parts. 'I'm not the one engaged to him, and dreaming about a mystery lover instead.'

Alex became agitated. 'I never said anything about the man in my dream being my lover.'

Julie chuckled. 'Fine. Then you won't mind telling me what the dream man was really like.'

Alex glared. 'Powerful,' she said, goaded.

Julie stared. There was something in the way Alex said it that brought up the hairs on the back of her neck. There was a long silence.

'That's all I can remember.' Alex swallowed. 'He was powerful. And I ran away from him.'

Julie shrugged. 'Well, if you ran away from him, there's nothing to be worried about, is there? Unless you didn't want to run away from him,' she added. 'Was he attractive, this guy?'

'Yes,' said Alex baldly.

'And you're sure you don't know him?'

Alex hesitated.

'You *do* know him. Wow.'

'No,' said Alex. 'I don't know him. But in the dream, I sort of thought I ought to.'

'Sounds as if you're right. Classic anxiety dream.' A nasty suspicion occurred to her. 'You and Rupert haven't set a date for marriage or done anything irrevocable, have you? Your repressed desires might be kicking against that, all right.'

Alex was exasperated. 'Look I didn't tell you so you could take a cheap shot at Rupert. Can't you see this has upset me?'

'Yes.' Julie was contrite. 'Sorry. But I can't believe you're making this fuss. It's so unlike you.'

'So is dreaming about men coming after me,' said Alex with irony. She heard what she had said and added with a grin, 'And if you say one word about wish fulfilment, I will pour that beer down your neck.'

Julie clutched the bottle to her breast. 'You probably ate too much cheese before you went to bed or something,' she said comfortingly. 'My guess is that the dream doesn't mean anything at all. Except that you had a bad night.'

'I expect you're right,' said Alex, after the tiniest pause. She pushed the coffee away from her. 'Anyway, there's nothing I can do about it. I'd better start getting ready.'

'Do you want me to do your hair?' offered Julie. Alex had dark, shoulder-length hair. At the best of times it waved thickly. After being caught in rain like today's, it was a mass of wild curls. 'Um ... it could do with a bit of tidying,' she added diplomatically.

Alex stood up. 'If I'm going to have anxiety dreams, why aren't they about hair turning into a briar hedge?' she said bitterly. 'Thanks. It obviously needs first aid. I'll give you a shout when I get out of the bath.'

Alex always had a long soak in warm, rose-scented water before she went out to a party. It made her relax. She needed that. She had a deep-seated fear of people in groups.

She had witnessed her parents' marriage break up over a succession of vicious dinner parties one London winter. She still got a clutch in her stomach when she remembered her mother's bright, false voice. Or her father's tight jaw. They had talked loudly. Circulated busily. But their hard, angry eyes had given them away. Now, whenever she went to a social gathering, Alex would look at people's eyes. Quite often they were chilling.

Julie did not understand, any more than her grandmother or any of her family did. Any more than Rupert did, really. But going to a party was still a real ordeal for Alex. And it was not getting any easier as she got older. Too often, recently, the rose-scented water had not done its work.

Well, it had better work tonight. This was her grandmother's big annual party. Tonight, Lavender had instructed Alex, she had to remember that she was a professional representative of Lavender Eyre and Associates. She had to look *radiant*.

It was going to take a lot of rose bath oil to do that, thought Alex.

Still, she applied herself methodically, as she always did.

The sophisticated clothes Lavender had sent her were not her taste, but they were beautiful. They would not make Alex look anything other than a short, round girl in a dress designed for a six-foot clothes' horse. But at least they would fit in among all the other designer dresses.

Finally, she squared up to her reflection in the dressing-table mirror, gazed at her heavy-lidded dark eyes and sighed. All the make-up in the world wouldn't turn her into a beauty or anything like it. Her eye shadow was too bright and looked uneven. And as for her lipstick … !

Julie came in, armed with her magic hair-box.

'You look gorgeous.'

'Lavender's dress looks gorgeous,' Alex corrected. 'I'm the usual fright. How do you avoid getting lipstick on your teeth?'

She had pinned her hair out of the way while she was bathing. Now Julie took the pins out and teased a comb through the tangles.

'Don't put yourself down all the time. You look great. Even Rupert will have to notice.'

'Rupert isn't going to be there.'

'Oh?' Julie was surprised.

'He has to work.'

'Oh.' Julie thought that Rupert had started to work rather a lot of evenings when he should have been with Alex. But she didn't say so. Alex had never commented when Julie's boyfriends neglected her, after all.

'No reason why he should be there. A banker among a lot of women talking about cosmetics. I shall be on duty, after all. And it's not as if I could spend any time with him.'

'Hey, you don't have to convince me.'

Julie experimented with a couple of swathes of hair. The great joy of Alex's mop was that, if you put it up, it stayed where it was put. She combed the next tress, saying through a mouthful of pins, 'So, who *will* be there?'

Alex ran through a guest list of the fashion aristocracy. 'Plus my mother, if she feels up to it, and Lavender's new walker. He's a wine merchant.' She paused, frowning in the mirror. 'And Joe Gomez.'

Julie was intrigued. She knew all about Joe Gomez. He had arrived in Alex's life twelve months ago like a tornado, and had been trying to scoop her up ever since. Ok, he wanted her to work for him – not go to bed with him – but at least it was a start, thought Julie. Rupert, the man with rights, hardly seemed to want Alex at all.

'It will be a nuisance, but Lavender insisted. She thinks he's cool. At least, when she doesn't think he's an American upstart who uses the wrong knife.'

Lavender was not only a tyrant, she was capricious with it. Alex spoke with affection, but Julie could detect weariness there. It must be hell trying to turn her grandmother's inspired spontaneity into some sort of consistent approach to business, thought Julie. And not getting much thanks for it either. Even Julie, spontaneous to her fingertips, could see that.

She was too kind to say so. She turned Alex's head a little so she could sculpt a wave of hair across her wide brow and said instead, 'She's right. The man's a dish.'

'I can't see it,' said Alex, still frowning horribly.

'Pure prejudice. He's got wonderful come-to-bed eyes. And his voice! When he did that thing on television, it just sent shivers up and down my spine.'

'You need therapy. I'm sure it's not healthy to have such a low lust threshold.'

'Just normal female appreciation.'

'Well, there'll be plenty of women there to appreciate him tonight. So I'm off the hook.'

'Some people just don't know their own luck.'

Alex said sharply, 'Joe Gomez is only interested in my professional skills, you know. We're not talking fairy stories here.'

Julie was working fast now, swirling hair and fixing it into place. In the mirror, Alex saw an intricate edifice of soft, shining hair start to frame her face. It softened the strong bones, making her eyes look deeper, her nape more tender. She looked younger, thought Alex, and vulnerable. She was not entirely sure she wanted to look vulnerable, but there was no doubt the result was pretty.

She turned her head, smiling. And stopped. Lying against her exposed nape was a corkscrew curl, gossamer fine but still there. She could feel it, just as she had felt it in her dream.

Suddenly, all her pleasure in the transformation evaporated. She was no longer sitting in her room, sharing laughter with her best friend. She was cold and alone, and trapped in a dream she did not understand. It was horrible and rather frightening.

Julie did not notice. She was packing up her magic hair-box, quite pleased.

'There you are. Fit for a princess.'

'Yes,' said Alex. She sounded rather alarmed.

Julie noticed that. She aimed a playful punch at the designer-silk shoulder.

'Go kill 'em, Sleeping Beauty.'

chapter two

'What happened?' asked Joe.

Tom Skelton had not slept for three nights, and looked it. Joe had been shocked when he walked into the pub.

Now he passed a hand over his face. 'I honestly don't know. They got the viewing figures in at once, of course. I thought they were pleased. They were better than I'd expected, anyway. It wasn't a high-profile slot. It hadn't had any trailing. No marketing push. Anyone who watched it was going to find it for themselves.'

Tom sounded like an automaton, thought Joe. As if he'd been going over and over it in his mind until he could not make sense of the words any more. He swore under his breath.

Tom did not hear him. The central London pub was noisy with commuters this early in the evening. Anyway, Tom was still locked into his compulsive monologue. 'But architecture has become fashionable, apparently.'

' "The new rock music",' quoted Joe, grinding his teeth.

Tom was surprised out of his trance. 'That's what Pendleton said.'

'He said it to me, too. Bloody shark.'

'Well, Pendleton read a review. They were good. You know they were good. So then he called for the audience response stuff. I sent you a copy, I thought you'd enjoy them. They were off the wall, but they weren't *bad*.' Tom shook his head.

Not for the first time, Joe reflected that his friend was surprisingly unworldly for a television producer. 'They were raves,' he said gently.

Tom looked even more unhappy. 'That's what I thought. But I must have been wrong. Pendleton called me in and said they weren't renewing my contract, and I was to go right away. In the middle of the week. At once.' He swallowed. 'I haven't told Sandra yet. I've been leaving the house every morning just as if I was going in to work, same as usual. But I'll have to. I've put my name out, but it will take time to find a new job. And I don't even know why I lost the last one.'

'I do,' said Joe. He was in a black rage.

Tom looked at him, torn between bewilderment and trepidation. 'Why?'

'Your idea was too good to come from someone who doesn't have the key to the executive wash-room,' Joe told him brutally. 'We are talking status and success here. Sorry, Tom, you're just not high enough up the food chain to get reviews like that.'

'Oh.' Tom digested it. 'I was never very good at politics,' he said ruefully, at last. 'That never occurred to me. Oh well, it's a shame, but that's that. It was a good idea.'

'It still is,' said Joe forcefully. He rummaged in his briefcase and brought out Pendleton's purple-and-gold folder. 'This is what they've dressed it up into. Doesn't mean much to me, but take a look.'

Tom didn't take it. 'No point. They won't take me back.'

'Not even if I make it a condition of my contract?'

Tom shook his head. 'Not once they've let me go. I know that much about politics. It would mean that Pendleton had made a mistake.'

Joe nodded. 'And Pendletons don't make mistakes, by definition. OK. That brings us to Plan B. I always preferred it anyway. In fact, that's why I asked you to meet me this evening.'

'What Plan B?'

'Your own production company,' said Joe excitedly. 'We make and market the series ourselves. There's hundreds of small production companies out there doing just that.'

Tom began to look alarmed. 'I'm no businessman, Joe.'

'All right, *our* production company.'

Tom laughed affectionately. 'You don't have the time. But thanks for thinking of it.'

Joe knew there was no point in pursuing it with Tom in this mood. They had waited tables together when Tom was at film school and Joe was arguing his way through a building surveyor's qualification. Tom, he knew, took time to assimilate new ideas. He sat back and snapped his briefcase shut.

'Talk it over with Sandy. I've got to go on somewhere this evening, anyway. We'll get together again next week. Meanwhile, are you OK for money?'

Tom had three children, the youngest not yet three months, and his wife was still on maternity leave.

'I'm fine. But thanks.'

They both looked the other way, embarrassed.

Tom changed the subject hurriedly, 'Where are you off to this evening, then? Guest of Honour at another ceremonial opening?'

Joe gave a crack of laughter. 'Not a chance. Lavender Eyre wouldn't allow me over the threshold if she didn't want me to do up her Palladian Mansion. No, Tom my boy, tonight I'm going hunting among the enemy.'

Tom laughed for the first time in days. 'You and your enemies,' he said affectionately. 'Who is it this time?'

'The English upper classes.'

'What have they done to you?'

Joe looked surprised. 'Me? Nothing. But they eat their children alive. I'm going to do something about it.'

Tom laughed until he cried. And then they had another beer. Then Tom said he might just have a look at Pendletons' folder, and think about whether there was any way he could put a team together. No promises. Just thinking.

Joe left, well satisfied.

The party was in full swing when Joe arrived. Lavender Eyre was standing in the elegant hallway talking to a group of high-fashion guests. She was a tiny woman. Wearing timeless Chanel and sapphires that matched her eyes, she looked like an ambassadorial hostess, not the successful businesswoman he knew her to be.

She came over as soon as she saw him.

'You're late,' she told him without preamble.

'Sorting out a small matter of fair play,' Joe said crisply. 'And before that, trying to put right one of my assistant's cock-ups, God help me. When are you going to stop being a dog in the manger about your wonderful granddaughter, and let me get my hands on her?'

Lavender gave him a haughty look and did not deign to answer.

Joe sighed. 'OK, OK. Do your own dirty work, Gomez.'

'Don't waste your breath. My granddaughter wouldn't look at you,' Lavender told him. 'She doesn't need to work, and she knows nothing about architecture.'

'But she knows about running a business.'

Lavender almost shuddered. 'Not your sort of business. You want someone who knows all the *nouveaux riches* who run the media these days. My Alex wouldn't know where to start.'

'Why the hell should I want a media babe?' asked Joe, so surprised he was not even offended.

Lavender sniffed. 'Everyone is talking about some appearance you made on television. Some of the comments have been downright salacious.'

Joe laughed down at her. 'Am I supposed to apologise for that?'

Lavender was a tyrant, a snob and as changeable as the wind, but she had a sense of humour. It was tickled now.

'I think you're supposed to use it,' she said dryly. 'Anyway, my friend, the media mogul's wife, made me promise to bring you over the moment you arrived.'

He raised his eyebrows. 'Media mogul's wife, eh? See, your Alex would know where to start, after all.'

Lavender stopped laughing. 'Don't even think about it, Gomez. Now, do you want to meet the media mogul, or not?'

Joe grinned. 'Lead on.'

The staircase was wide and shallow. She took him up, nodding to people conversing on the stairs as she passed.

'You're looking very good,' she said approvingly. Appearance was crucial to Lavender.

'Thank you,' said Joe, taken aback.

She stopped for a moment and surveyed him dispassionately.

'Of course you're tall. That counts for a lot on television, I'm told. Alex,' she added, without a pause, 'doesn't like tall men. She says it gives her a crick in her neck when she talks to them.'

She resumed climbing the stairs.

Joe paced with her, imitating a wolfish prowl. 'No problem. It wasn't talking I had in mind.'

Lavender was unmoved. 'Amusing,' she said without cracking a smile. 'Say it to Alex and she'll run a mile.'

'I know,' he said, abandoning the feral expression.

'No you don't,' said Alex's grandmother. 'You think she can handle anything. And you're wrong.'

His lips twitched. 'She handles you,' he pointed out.

Lavender did not like that. 'Oh, you think you're so charming. Do your worst,' she said irritably. 'It won't get you anywhere with Alex. She is loyal.'

They were at the stop of the stairs. She led the way into her office. The emphasis on the rococo was enhanced by four uplighters focusing on the ornate ceiling. A huge flower arrangement stood in a marble urn on the mantelpiece.

'Over there.'

Joe looked. 'I can't see Alex.'

Lavender clicked her tongue. 'Not Alex. Media Mogul and wife.' She added naughtily, 'Take care. She was very impressed by how you looked in a ripped shirt.'

Joe pulled a face. And then he had an idea.

Tom Skelton needed a backer, or his great idea would be hijacked by an expert parasite. It was unjust, and Joe had a veritable passion for justice. Such a passion, in fact, that he turned the full battery of his charm on the woman, while he pitched Tom's idea, even more charmingly, to her husband. But even while he worked the encounter for all he was worth, he was scanning the crowd out of the corner of his eye.

She was here somewhere – his target, his prize, his Alex.

She knew Joe had arrived when the woman columnist she was talking to said, 'Who is *that?*'

Alex did not even try to see over the crowd. But she knew Diana Holding, and she knew she did not get excited easily.

'Tall, dark and deadly?'

'And how!' agreed Diana.

'That's my grandmother's dark angel,' she said with feeling.

The columnist gave a crow of laughter. 'Well, good for Lavender. Gives hope to a woman in her mere fifties.'

Alex frowned. 'Not that sort of angel. You've got a filthy mind, Diana.'

'And yours could do with coming out of its packaging,' said Diana frankly. 'Don't go puritan on me, Alex darling. Tell me where Lavender found the hunk. He's scrummy.'

'He found *her*. They've got this terrible project going to restore the old family pile together. He's an architect.'

Diana snapped her fingers. 'That's where I've seen him before. On the box, last week. He was climbing all over some rocks, talking about keystones and rippling his muscles.'

'You're drooling,' said Alex coldly.

'I'm just wishing I had a ruined folly he could come and restore for me,' said Diana frankly. '*Clever* Lavender.'

Alex hesitated. But Diana was a long-standing friend of the family.

'It's a complete pain,' Alex said, in a spurt of unusual temper. 'It's going to cost her a fortune, even if she gets Joe to do the plans for nothing. Which, frankly, I doubt. He knows she can afford it, and he doesn't like the upper classes.'

'Wow,' said Diana, impressed.

'We had a day there in the summer. Joe talking about Palladian symmetry and the cost of restoration. Lavender talking about what fun it would be to have a self-help project, so we could all get back in touch with our creative selves.'

'Holy cow. That sounds like a game-and-a-half.'

'It was hell on wheels. Mother came too, and cried because she said she could see Dad's house between the trees,'

'Could she?'

'Not without a crystal ball. There's three miles of woodland between them. But of course, my father heard what was going on, so he brought the dogs down and patrolled the perimeter like a born-again security guard.'

Diana looked at her with a good deal of sympathy.

'You're not lucky in your parents.'

Alex sighed. 'There's nothing wrong with either of them, individually. They just hate each other. And Lavender siding with Mother against Dad, her own son, has added enough fuel to keep the fire going forever.'

Diana gave her a quick hug. 'Poor old Alex. The life of the peacemaker is not easy.'

Alex started to push a hand through her hair, remembered Julie's complex handiwork and rubbed her brow instead.

'Don't listen to me, Di. I've had a bad week. Dad is pressurising me to go to a dance he wants to give for my half-sister, Laine, and Mother's thrown a wobbly. A "How can you go to the house, now he's installed That Woman there" sort of thing. I say it's not Laine's fault. Hell, she *is* my half-sister. But you know Mother when she starts to feel rejected. She's gone reclusive. And now I'm having bad dreams.'

'I'm not surprised.'

That cheered Alex up as nothing else had, ever since she'd woken up that morning.

'No, I suppose it's not all that surprising, is it?' she said. 'Between Mum and Dad and this blasted dance.'

'Don't tell me your father's into moral blackmail too,' said Diana, amused.

'Oh no. Dad's just furious. It's the money, really. That's what he's so mad about. Hope Place, the family's huge Palladian mansion, is practically falling down. He could never afford even to make it liveable in. So, I said, what does it matter what Lavender does to it? It isn't as if she's going to turn it into a transport café. Joe has gone right back to the original plans. It's a historical reconstruction. It will probably break the bank by the time they're finished, too. But Dad just went wild and said it was the principle of the thing. That Granddad should never have broken up the estate and left it to her.'

'Territory. You've got to be sorry for him.'

'I'm stuck in the middle. I'm not feeling sorry for anyone,' said Alex grimly.

'Not even the hunk?'

Alex stuck her nose in the air. 'Least of all the hunk. He started it.'

'Oh come on, Alex. It's not his fault your family are crazy. You can't blame the poor guy for the family feud.'

Alex was essentially fair-minded. Her nose came down and she sighed.

'No, I know I can't. I just wish he hadn't stirred it all up again, that's all. Things were on a reasonably even keel until Joe Gomez stuck his oar in.'

She frowned, thinking about the latest exchange of vitriolic phonecalls. Now, if she was going to have nightmares, why on earth had she not had nightmares about screaming parents?

Diana stared at her. 'Don't you like him?'

Alex came out of her brown study with a jump. 'Who? Joe? Sure. When he's not setting my family at war, he's a great guy.'

Diana's eyes widened. 'A great guy?' she echoed faintly.

'Well, he's got a nasty sense of humour and he likes to tease. But apart from that, he's OK.'

'OK?' gasped Diana. '*OK?*'

'Yes. So what?'

'The man,' said Diana with restraint, 'is not just "OK". Look at him. Look at everyone else looking at him. Intelligence, muscles *and* he looks like something out of a dream you would be ashamed to tell your grandmother.'

Alex grinned suddenly. 'Not me. If I told my grandmother about a dream like that, she'd jump for joy.'

Diana gave up. 'You're unnatural.'

'I'm an engaged woman.'

Well, it was almost true. 'We'd better get married,' Rupert had said at Easter. He had not mentioned it since, but Alex knew that it would happen one day. She could wait. When you had loved someone as long as she had loved Rupert, waiting was what you did well.

Diana was shaking her head with disapproval. 'I've been happily married for twenty years. Doesn't stop me looking.'

'Ah, but you're a rule-breaker, and I'm not,' teased Alex.

A waiter appeared at her elbow. 'Sorry, Diana, I'll have to slide off and see what's happening in the kitchen. People are drinking faster and eating slower than we expected.'

Diana waved her champagne flute. 'Go and do your duty,' she said. 'Just like always.'

Alex smiled as if she did not quite understand her and eased her way through the crowd. No point in defending herself to Diana, she thought. Besides, it was true. She did do her duty and keep to the rules. She had first-hand evidence of what happened when you didn't. An only child caught in a marriage duel had a ringside seat, thought Alex sadly.

So, true to form, she worked hard through the rest of the party.

By nine o'clock, Lavender was looking finely drawn. Not tired. She would never admit to 'tired'. But now she wanted to go home and put her feet up.

'It's OK. I'll clear up and see the caterers out,' said Alex.

To her surprise, Joe Gomez appeared at her elbow. He said, 'I'll give you a hand.'

To her even greater surprise, her grandmother said, 'Would you, Joe? That would be a weight off my mind.'

It sounded as if she meant it, too.

'What's wrong?' she said, tucking Lavender into her chauffeured limousine.

Lavender closed the door, then pressed the button to lower the window. She put out a claw-like hand to take Alex's.

'I hoped your mother would be there,' she said with apparent irrelevance.

'Probably forgot. Or decided everyone would hate her. You know mother.'

'Yes. Yes. I do.'

'I'll call her. I'm sure she's fine,' said Alex reassuringly. 'But I can drop by on my way home, if you like.'

'No,' said Lavender with sudden strength. 'No, you do too much already. Your mother is my responsibility. It was my son who got her into this mess in the first place. Time I did something about it.'

She patted Alex's cheek with an uncharacteristic gesture. Lavender was not given to shows of affection.

'You're a good girl. Don't let Joe bully you.'

Before Alex could demand an explanation of this obscure piece of advice, she had tapped the chauffeur on the shoulder and the car pulled away.

'Weird,' Alex told the night sky.

But she did not tell Joe Gomez anything at all.

She did not know why her grandmother thought that Joe might try to bully her and, until she did, she was not going to risk putting the thought into his head. Of course, he would never succeed. Alex knew something about resisting bullies. Still, there was no point in letting him think it might be worth trying.

She knew quite well that Joe wanted her to work for him. He had been trying for ages. She knew the exact moment it had started, too.

He had come round to see Lavender about restoring the old family home, Hope Place, one day in the spring. It was just before they'd published the company's annual results, and it had not been a good year. Recriminations flew. The external auditor took a pasting and retired, hurt.

And that was the trouble. Seeing the auditor totter out into the street, Lavender's hitherto flawless secretary had concluded that the meeting was over. So when Joe turned up with a roll of plans under his arm, she had not stopped him breezing into Lavender's office.

He had walked into a maelstrom. Gerald Miller, the Managing Director, was red in the face and shouting. The Head of Research was wringing his hands. A clutch of international representatives was babbling complaints, excuses and suggestions. Lavender, herself, was speechless with fury for once. The other voices in the room had risen to storm force.

And then Alex rose to her feet.

'Maybe we can find a way through this,' she said quietly. 'Everyone has one sentence to say what their first priority for the annual statement is. Only one sentence. Only one priority. Lavender, you first.'

And suddenly, they all had hope.

The voices calmed. Gerald's colour returned to normal.

Lavender said something, but Alex never remembered what. Because Joe had been standing in the doorway, transfixed. He looked amused, wondering, enchanted. 'I'm in love,' he had said.

Alex ignored him then. She ignored him later. And she went on ignoring him, even when he bombarded her with hot-house flowers and passionately worded offers of employment. She ignored him when he was a fellow guest at one of Lavender's dinners, and kept whispering astronomical salary offers in her ear.

'There are lots of office managers like me in London,' she told him. 'Find one.'

'But I want you.'

'No you don't. You just want to prove you can get me,' she said shrewdly.

He had laughed, buffed her cheek with a pretend punch and admitted it.

But it did not stop him. Was he going to have another go tonight?

She watched him warily. But he did not mention a word about her changing jobs. Instead, he hauled furniture back into place, and was generally a pillar of strength. He even helped the caterers carry cases of empty bottles out to their waiting van.

Alex tipped the waiters, said goodnight and locked the front door.

'All done?' said Joe.

'I just need to put the rest of the cash back in the safe. One last check and I'm on my way.'

She went upstairs. He kept pace with her.

'I'll drive you home.'

'No need. It's not that late. I'll pick up a cab in Piccadilly easily.'

He was not listening. 'In fact, I'll do better than that. You must be starving. I'll buy you dinner.'

Here it comes, thought Alex.

'No, thank you.'

She went into the big room, now restored to the spacious tranquillity of the Chairman's office. He followed her.

'I'd like to. You've worked like a dog tonight. You deserve it.'

'Don't be too noble, Joe,' she said tartly. 'It doesn't go down well, especially when I know you've got a contract in your pocket.'

He looked wounded. 'You don't think I'd try to take advantage of woman on the brink of exhaustion?'

'I think you'd take any advantage you could get,' Alex told him frankly. 'And …'

But what she was going to say next was lost as she skidded on a fallen asparagus canapé. It squashed, causing her to skid. Joe Gomez fielded her.

There was an odd, breathless moment that Alex did not understand. She leaned back against his sustaining arm and looked up into his suddenly narrowed eyes.

'Any advantage I can get, hmm?' mused Joe wickedly.

'Joe …'

She was thrown off balance in his arms. Alex did not like the feeling. She put out a hand to steady herself. Somehow, she must have knocked the up-lighter. It wavered on its stalk and then, with a loud pop, every light in the room went out.

Joe laughed. He did not let her go. She could feel the laughter under his ribs, in his throat. It felt amazingly intimate. Shockingly intimate.

Alex had never allowed herself to imagine being this intimate with Joe Gomez. She realised, appalled, that that was over now. From this moment on, it would always be there, that imaginative possibility. Even if they never did anything about it. Even if she never let herself think about it again.

She had admitted that the attraction was there. Admitted it

now, tonight, on pure instinct, without thinking about it. And she would never now be able to tell herself she had not.

A sea change was starting. There was not a thing she could do to halt it. But she could try.

'This is not going to happen,' she said with determination.

Panting, she tore herself away. Joe laughed again. In naked panic, Alex fled to the window, not quite as dark as the rest of the room.

He followed.

What was happening? She thought wildly. Joe was a friend. Always amusing, generally reliable, infinitely challenging, he was a constant. She knew the way he thought, the way he worked.

But she did not know him as the silent-footed predator who came to her across tumbled furniture. She did not know the man who brushed aside her own blank retreat. She did not know the man who aroused her into wakefulness.

Perhaps it had something to do with the dark. The sodium glare from outside picked out grotesque shadows from everyday objects, that Alex knew as well as she knew herself. As well as she thought she knew Joe.

Or perhaps it was the unnatural quiet. For a moment, it was as if Joe had stepped into one of her own dreams, where anything was possible; anything permissible.

Her dreams. *Her dreams…*

'Oh God,' said Alex, under her breath. She was trembling so much she could hardly stand.

But when he came to her, she still lifted her hands to his face and gave him kiss for frantic kiss.

Joe lifted his head. His eyes glinted down at her like black mineral in an underground cavern. In the dark, they were quite unreadable.

Was he disconcerted by her response? Shocked by her passion? Embarrassed (oh, agony) by her abandon? Alex could not tell.

Her hands fell.

He held her breast to breast, scanning her face in the near dark. Alex was trembling, not just in her limbs but in her whole being, from her heart to her temples. She felt strange, as if she would not recognise herself if she looked in the mirror.

'Joe.' Her voice was strange too, as if her vocal chords had furred over. He did not answer; or not with words. Instead he took her face gently between his hands and feathered his lips over her features, like a blind man learning the terrain by touch. It occurred to her, astonishingly, that he was trembling too.

She said in a husky voice, 'Joe, please, I can't …'

He did not let her finish. He stopped dead for a moment, as if recalled to an unwelcome reality. And then his hands were no longer gentle, and his mouth became demanding.

The silent room was made strange by shadows. Nothing felt stranger than to be in Joe's arms as they kissed like two lovers.

Oh yes, there was no pretending about that. They felt like lovers. They touched like lovers. They explored each other's mouths like lovers made savage by absence.

So there was no pretending, even to herself, that he was kissing her against her will. Even as she whimpered with newly awakened desire, Alex admitted it.

She was as savage as he. And as hungry.

I didn't know, she thought, clumsy with need. *I didn't know.*

She did not know how long they stood there, locked together, almost desperate. She did know that, in the end, it was Joe who drew back.

That shocked her more than all the rest. The moment his hands fell, she backed away, appalled.

'Oh hell.' She was nearly weeping. She rubbed the back of her hand across her mouth like a frightened child. 'What have I done?'

Joe went very still. Alex had a sudden feeling she had hurt him mortally. It had to be nonsense of course, but she was already reaching out to him in spontaneous remorse, when he said coolly, 'Nothing irretrievable.' Alex's hand fell. 'I'm sorry …'

She did not know what she was apologising for, unless it was for embarrassing him. For invading his mouth as if she had the right. For tearing at his clothes so that his shirt was now crazily awry. She could see the way it sagged, even in the half-dark. If anyone had walked in on them now, that shirt alone would tell its own tale. She buried her face in her hands.

He made a sharp movement, cutting her off.

She stood there, helpless.

He said softly, 'Not half as sorry as I am.'

Alex flinched. There was no doubt that he meant it.

'Time you were home and I was … anywhere else.'

Alex felt stupid. She said with difficulty, 'The fuse box. I need to get the lights sorted out.'

He gave a harsh laugh. 'The perfect administrator. Of course you do. And you don't need any help, either, do you?'

She drew careful breaths. She could not bear it if he knew how shocked she was. Or how close she had come to dragging him to the floor and …

She cut the thought off abruptly. 'I think I can handle that, thank you.'

It was the professional Alex; cool, unflappable, practical Alex who could find the answer to any problem.

The Alex he had once said he was in love with.

She flinched, in the dark. There was no point in remembering him saying that. It was a joke, she told herself. A joke at the time, and a joke now. Only a joke. Like everything else that had happened this evening.

'OK,' said Joe. 'You go right ahead and handle it. I'd just hate to get in your way.'

It was impossible to imagine him ever saying he was in

love with her again, thought Alex. Just as well, in the circumstances, of course. So why did she feel so horribly let down?

'Goodbye,' she said in her nicest, good-girl voice.

Joe said dangerously, 'Alex, if you offer to shake hands with me, I won't be responsible.'

She jumped back, as if she was scalded.

'And don't look so scared,' he jeered. 'You stamped out the fire all on your own. You can handle anything.'

He paused. But Alex said nothing.

Joe did not trust himself to touch her again. He crashed the door behind him.

chapter three

The house was in darkness when Alex got home. Julie was not
back. Alex let herself in and stood in the hall for a moment
without putting the light on.

She felt very lonely. It scared her. She had never felt lonely
in her own house before.

She loved her home. She had loved it from the moment she
bought it and had set about decorating the place to make it
utterly her own. She had never let herself in and stood in the
dark, feeling as if she was on a ship that was about to hit an
iceberg before. Home was *safe*. Hers and safe.

She pursed her lips, gave herself a shake and put on the
light.

Coffee, she thought. Coffee and perhaps a fire, for the
autumn night was chilly. She walked through the sitting room,
snapping on table lamps and flaming the gas fire. Half an hour
tucked up in front of the fire with a good novel, and she would
feel human again.

It was stupid to be so ruffled by a kiss. Joe Gomez had not
been ruffled. Well, he had been annoyed. But Alex knew
about annoyance. She knew the difference between that and
the diamond-hard note that meant furious feeling. She had
heard that too often in her father's voice to mistake it.

In fact, Joe Gomez had probably forgotten it already. He
would probably laugh aloud if he could see her now. He
would never have guessed that his teasing would upset her so
much. He would think she was an independent woman who
could handle it, just as she had said she was. Though, of
course, he should have known better than to take his social
teasing to that extreme.

She put on the kettle.

Yes, that was better. Concentrate on how badly Joe had behaved. Then she might forget her own tremulous response.

That was the real shocker, thought Alex. Her response.

She was in love with Rupert. She had been in love with Rupert since she was six. Everyone knew it. She had never looked at anyone else. Never thought of falling in love with anyone else. So how on earth could she have reacted to Joe Gomez's kiss like a lovesick groupie?

She drew a ragged breath.

She had kissed him back. More than kissed. *Why?*

It should have been so easy to draw away, step back, smile and say, 'No, thank you'. She had done it so many times, to so many men. What was different about Joe Gomez?

Or was it the situation? The sheer surprise of it? She had not quite believed it when he reached for her. Yes, that had to be it.

Not quite believing it, she had not quite fended him off. And so Joe must have thought that she wanted his kiss when she did not. She just gave out the wrong signals.

Mistake, of course. Mistake and surprise and . . .

'Tell the truth,' Alex told herself harshly. 'You wanted it. You might not have expected it, but you wanted it, all right. You weren't fighting him off. And not because you'd gone into shock, either. Not even when you fused the lights.'

Alex winced. If Joe Gomez thought she had encouraged him tonight, she had no one but herself to blame.

The kettle, overfilled, spat boiling water across the counter.

'*Damn,*' said Alex aloud, not entirely at the spillage.

She splashed the hot water onto coffee granules.

Just as well Rupert isn't here, she thought. Rupert hated instant coffee. In fact Rupert hated anything that was cheap and convenient. Rupert liked her to make a proper ceremony over the things she did for him, and making real coffee was all part of it.

She took the steaming mug back into the sitting room and sank onto the rug in front of the fire.

Rupert.

Oh, he should have been there tonight. She should have insisted. Only …he'd looked so blank when she asked him. His displeasure had felt like a cold wind blowing in from a suddenly opened door. Even in front of her fire now, Alex shivered when she thought about it.

The trouble is, I know too much about the withdrawal of love, she thought sadly, which reminded her of her mother. She had meant to drop in on her on her way home. Damn! Oh well, a phone call would have to do.

Caroline Eyre answered at the third ring, which was surprising. Often, she hid behind her answering machine.

'Hello, Alex. How was your party?'

Alex had got out of the habit of telling her mother her troubles a long, long time ago.

Now she said brightly, 'Oh, fine. Lots of people asked after you. Diana was there.'

'Nice,' said her mother. 'Did Rupert enjoy himself?'

Ouch. Why hadn't she thought that her mother was bound to ask about Rupert? Ever since her own marriage had collapsed, she was almost obsessive about Alex managing to acquire and hold on to a husband of her own. She had welcomed the news of their informal engagement with almost hysterical relief.

'He was working. Couldn't make it.'

Caroline Eyre's voice went up several notches. 'You aren't doing anything silly, are you, Alex?'

Define silly, thought Alex dryly. *I got kissed stupid by a man I find a lot more attractive than I ought to.*

Aloud she said, 'No, I'm not doing anything silly, mother. People just don't live in each other's pockets any more.'

Caroline was not reassured. 'Is anything wrong between you?'

No, no more than usual, thought Alex patiently. *Rupert doesn't say he loves me, and I can't relax when he holds me. And we do the best we can. He takes me out every Friday night and I pretend that I want to make love, because if I do, maybe he will say he loves me one day.* The thought shocked her. She had never thought that before.

She said hastily, 'No, there's nothing wrong. We've known each other for so long, it's bound to be a bit dull sometimes. No surprises left.'

'Be grateful for it,' said Caroline. And began to cry.

Oh lord, thought Alex. She banished her own disquietude and went into comforting-counsellor mode. 'What is it, mother?' she said kindly.

But her mother would not stop crying.

So, Alex did what she had done so many times before: pulled on her outdoor clothes; went out into the rainy streets to find a taxi; took it to her mother's pretty Mayfair apartment; listened.

Caroline had not been outside her flat in four days. Her great Chinese urns were full of dead flowers, and the fridge was full of uneaten food going rotten. Alex threw everything away and cleared out the kitchen. Then, she made her mother some warm broth and put her to bed.

'You've got to stop this,' she said gently. 'You're a young woman yet. You've got to get out and do something with your life.'

'What?' said Caroline. She had stopped crying, but she looked as drained as Alex was feeling.

'Voluntary work. A job. Anything.'

'I'm not trained for anything except being a wife and mother,' said Caroline, her eyes filling again. 'When your father left, he took my job away from me.'

'Stop it,' said Alex, kindly but with great firmness. 'That was a long time ago. There are plenty of things you can do. Talk to Lavender. She has hundreds of friends who work for charities. In fact, she was saying something like that this evening. When she calls, why don't you ask her if she can find you something?'

She kissed her mother good night. Caroline clung to her for a moment.

'And you and Rupert really are all right?'

'We're fine, mother,' Alex reassured her.

But she shivered as if she was out in the cold again. A nasty little voice in her head said, *As long as I go on pretending.*

It was only when she was home in bed, with her eyes dropping drowsily as she snuggled under the warm duvet, that she thought, *When Joe kissed me, it wasn't pretending.* But by then she was too close to sleep to notice.

What a disaster, thought Joe. *You've really blown it this time.*

He had never made a woman cry with just a kiss before. Joe was trying hard to see the funny side of last night's encounter. It was not easy.

He was pounding around the running track in the morning mist. Now that he had warmed up, his arms and legs moved like pistons, and his breathing was regular. So that had easily reasserted discipline over his muscles, Joe thought with satisfaction. Pity he could not whip his thoughts into line at the same time.

Or, even better, last night.

What had possessed him? He knew Alex Eyre by now. He knew how she reacted to being touched. Again and again, he had seen her step back at a too-pressing embrace. Even that idiot she claimed to be engaged to barely brushed her lips when they met. And Joe Gomez, flirtation expert of the western world, had to kiss the life half out of her.

You'd think he was a high-school kid on a hormone surge. What the hell had come over him?

And yet …And yet …She had not stepped back from *him*. Joe Gomez, flirt of the western world, had achieved that at least. For a moment there, last night, she had been with him every step of the way.

Remembering how far that way had gone, the even pace of his breathing quickened. Out of synchronisation suddenly, his feet faltered. Joe missed a step. There was a precarious moment when one foot kicked the other and the track tilted to a dangerous angle.

He righted himself. He was too alert, too physically in control, to allow himself to trip on an empty track. But he was shaken. He had never done anything like that, not since he first started running seriously all those years ago in the Atlas Mountains.

Back then, the track had been treacherous with stones. He had been less than twelve, a gangly boy, taller than his pugnacious father, all arms and legs and bad attitude. But even then, when rebellion had driven him out on to the mountainside and only fury had kept him there, he had always been sure-footed as a goat. In the intervening years, his co-ordination had only sharpened. He simply did not fall over while he was running.

Of course, he had never before let the image of Alex Eyre come running with him. Particularly not an Alex who had melted surprisingly into his arms. An Alex who had kissed him in return. Kissed him so hard, in fact, that for a moment he …

He stumbled and nearly took a dive.

'Shit!' said Joe aloud. He brought himself to a halt.

This had got to stop. He ran on the spot, trying to get back the rhythm of his breathing. It did not come.

There was no point in running any more, he admitted ruefully. His imaginary Alex was not going to go away. And he was going to end up having to explain away a series of undignified bruises. That was, if he did not actually tear something.

He jogged carefully back to the changing rooms.

While he was doing his wind-down stretches, Tom turned

up. Joe was not entirely surprised, as Tom knew he ran here every morning.

'You must have started early,' said Tom, surprised.

'Yes.'

Joe was not going to admit to anyone else that he had cut his training run short. Tom might ask why. He was not prepared to answer that yet, if ever.

Instead, he shook out his muscles in the usual sequence, just as if he had completed this morning's session on target. He took off his running shoes and socks, and went over to his sports bag.

'I'm glad you dropped by. I bumped into someone last night who might be interested.'

The media mogul had given him his business card. Joe fished in his wallet and brought it out, then flipped it to Tom.

'Know him?'

Tom read the name and looked up surprised. 'He's a network man. He doesn't make programmes. He schedules them.'

'So? That's what we need, isn't it. You can *make* the stuff. We need someone to sell it.'

'And fund it,' said Tom. 'Where will the capital come from?'

'Me,' said Joe. 'Him. Maybe a couple of others who think it's a good idea. Bank loan to top up.'

Tom's jaw worked. 'It's a big step.'

Joe was pulling his sports shirt over his head. 'Whatever you do now will be a big step, Tom. You're a man with three children and no job.' He picked up his towel and headed for the showers.

'The real Gomez. He tells it like it is,' said Tom, following.

'That's me. Never pays to run from the truth.'

Joe got under the shower and began to soap vigorously, scrubbing shampoo into his hair with a pitiless hand.

'This guy last night,' he said, eyes tight shut against the

cascade. 'He says the most important thing is to make a calling card episode. You can use *Palaces and Pigpens*.'

'But . . .'

'Take it along to see him. He's already heard about it. His wife had raved to him about it. Very useful.'

'But Gryphon bankrolled that programme. Can I legally use their work to sell my own?'

'You directed it,' said Joe. 'It's your work.' He rinsed off the shampoo and the rest of the soap before turning off the water and reaching for the towel.

'That's better,' he said calmly. 'Now, I don't know what your legal position is. Go and see your lawyer. I'll pick up the tab, if they ask. But I'd be surprised if anyone can stop you using an idea they haven't paid you for.'

He towelled briskly and got into today's work clothes. He had a meeting with a big corporate at eleven, so it was the tailored suit today. Joe preferred jeans and heavy boots, because that meant it was a day he would be scrambling around on site, making his creation come to life. But if he had to wear smart, he was *smart*. Today, it was a graphite-grey jacket that moulded his shoulders like a second skin and indulged him with a silk-lined waistcoat. Joe liked waistcoats.

'Play-actor!' Tom said, amused, watching Joe undo the bottom button of the waistcoat before putting on that perfection of a jacket.

'I like to dress the part,' agreed Joe.

He settled the jacket, flicked his cuffs into place and tidied his hair. He did it all without once looking in any of the mirrors around the changing room. Joe might be a play-actor, but he is not vain, Tom thought.

Joe stuffed the towel into his sports bag and turned to the door. Then he looked back.

'Don't lie down under this, Tom. You're a good director. We can lick these bastards at their own game.'

'Gomez the Crusader strikes again,' said Tom gruffly.

'Thank you.' He swallowed. 'What can I say? I never thought
. . .'

'Hey, life is what happens when you're making other plans,
right? Don't thank me. Fight back.'

They went out into the cool morning together. The running
track was in the middle of a municipal park. They had both
left their cars in the peripheral car park.

Tom said curiously, 'You always fight back, don't you?'

'Always,' said Joe calmly.

'And it always works?'

Joe laughed. 'Come on, Tom. Get real. I've been knocked
back sometimes, sure.'

'And you don't care? About the reverses, I mean.'

'Reverses are what make you fight harder,' Joe said with
relish.

There were only a few cars in the car park. No prizes for
guessing which was Joe's, thought Tom. He had parked his
littered and grubby family hatchback next to it as soon as he
saw its gleaming lines.

Sure enough, Joe unlocked the door of the silver sports car
and threw his bag across onto the passenger seat.

'Not too many reverses, by the look of it,' Tom said dryly.
'Nice car.' He stroked the sleek nose. 'Pull a lot of birds with
this one?'

For a moment Joe looked at him blankly. Then he shook his
head, mouth wry. 'Not the one that matters.'

Tom stared at him in clear disbelief.

Joe grinned. 'Thank you, Tom. That's more encouragement
than I've had all year.' He swung himself into the low car,
pressed a button to lower the window and looked up at Tom,
all laughter banished. 'Go for it.'

'I will,' said Tom. 'I'll call the lawyer now.' A thought
occurred to him. 'Hey, I could end the day with my own production company.'

'Quite right' said Joe with enthusiasm. 'See you.'

He gunned the engine and was off.

Tom shook his head. Who on earth was the woman who could resist both a silver Jensen Healey and Joe Gomez? He had never heard Joe mention a special woman before. And why in hell's name was she turning down all that energy and drive and sheer masculine power?

Women, thought Tom, getting back into his own car and switching on his mobile phone, were simply incomprehensible.

'Women don't do this sort of thing,' said Alex quietly.

She was fighting for her life, and getting quieter and quieter. She heard herself and despaired. What was wrong with her? Why couldn't she even raise her voice when her whole career was at stake?

Lavender was looking guilty, but mulish. It was a lethal combination. It meant she knew she was in the wrong, and was going to go ahead anyway.

Alex said, 'It's men who kick people out with no warning. Women managers are supposed to seek consensus.'

Lavender stuck her chin in the air. 'Twaddle! Managers do what managers have to. Men or women, it makes no difference.'

'So why do you think you have to sack me?'

Inside, she was gnashing her teeth with fury and worse, but her voice was still level. *Good old Alex!* she thought bitterly. *Never make a scene! Let yourself be argued into oblivion, all over again!*

Lavender hesitated. Then she said in a pugnacious tone, 'You don't need the job. Your mother does.'

Alex stared. '*Mother?* But she never puts her nose outside the flat these days.'

'Quite.'

'You're giving her my job – *my* job – as a sort of therapy?' said Alex in disbelief.

Lavender's eyes narrowed to slits. 'You told her to talk it over with me. It's clear to me she needs a challenge.'

'You're crazy!'

'Don't you think she needs a challenge then?'

'Yes, of course she does. A challenge – not total annihilation!' She leaned forward, hands on Lavender's rococo desk, and hissed, 'You listen to me, Grandma. I'm not just here for decoration, you know. I *run* this place.'

Lavender tossed her head like a blue-rinsed five-year-old, but she said nothing.

Alex straightened. 'You have your ideas,' she said in that steady, unemotional voice she used to cool heated board discussions. 'Geoffrey makes sure they're profitable. But *I'm* the one that delivers. Shipments go where they're supposed to, ad campaigns start on time, questions get answered, because of *me*. Do you really think mother will be able to handle that?'

Lavender's chin went even higher. 'With a bit of help. As long as you leave her proper notes.'

'How on earth can I do that?'

'Well, if you're going to be spiteful . . .'

Alex flung herself away from the rococo desk. She went over to the window and looked down into the street.

'You don't understand,' she said in frustration. 'I'm a trouble-shooter. I do whatever comes up. I can do it because I know the business so well. I can't just strip out everything I know from my brain and leave it on a diskette.'

Lavender said, 'Well, she'll just have to do what you did, when I took you on. Find her own way around.'

Alex closed her eyes briefly. 'But the company was tiny then.'

'My mind is made up,' Lavender said in the flat voice that Alex knew so well. 'Your mother is heading for a nervous breakdown, or whatever they call it these days. My son did it to her. It's up to me to put it right. I need to get her going again. And I never will if you're here, showing her how inadequate she is.'

Alex spun round, shocked. 'I wouldn't.'

'Alex my dear, you'd do it with the first telephone call you answered,' said Lavender brutally. 'Anyway, it's time you spread your wings. Take a year out. Travel. Go to the States and get some work experience there.'

It was Alex's turn to narrow her eyes. 'This is about breaking me up from Rupert, isn't it?' she said, enlightened.

Lavender shrugged. 'If your relationship with Rupert isn't strong enough to handle a year's separation . . .' she said airily. She waved a hand to disclaim any further responsibility.

Quite suddenly Alex stopped being reasonable. 'Fine,' she said. She went to the door.

For the first time in the interview, Lavender showed signs of agitation. She stood up. 'What are you going to do?'

'Get another job,' said Alex furiously.

It was the last thing Lavender expected. She blinked. 'But you can't.'

'Watch me.'

'You've got a contract.'

'You should have thought of that earlier.'

'I was thinking about your mother,' said Lavender tragically. 'She *needs* me.'

'And I need a job. OK, I accept that I don't need it financially. I need it for my self-respect.'

Lavender's eyes slid away from hers. 'Not as much as your mother does.'

Alex did not soften. 'OK. I'll go work for someone else.'

The concerned mother-in-law was suddenly swamped by the acute businesswoman. 'If you try to go to any of our rivals – I'll sue them stupid,' said Lavender grimly.

'Now who's being spiteful?'

'Alex . . .'

Alex put her hands on her hips. 'Do I keep my job?'

Lavender glared. 'No, you don't. This is my company, and I'll do what I want.'

'Right,' said Alex, in a deceptively amiable voice. 'Good-bye.'

She banged the door shut behind her and ran down the staircase so fast that she nearly missed her footing. She was shaking. How dare Lavender! Oh, how *dare* she?

Alex did not hesitate outside her office. She ran straight out into the street, breathing hard.

The autumnal sun had turned the stucco buildings to gold. She did not notice. She stamped along the elegant row of houses, furious and unseeing.

I know what you're doing, she said to Lavender in her head. *You think you can kill two birds with one stone. Make a success of Mother and a failure of my engagement. Great thinking, Lavender. But it's not going to work.*

The Regency terrace led off to a wooded square. Now a gust of wind whirled some leaves along the pavement ahead of her that must have fallen since the street cleaner's morning round. The brittle sound of crunching leaves brought her up short. It sounded, for a moment, like the crackle of flames. Something prompted her memory.

The sound of flames...wind...the deserted street of Regency houses... *The dream.*

Alex shivered violently, but it had nothing to do with the cold.

Pure coincidence, she argued with herself. The dream was set at night. What was more, it had the trappings of pure Jane Austen, from the flambeaux outside the front door to her own corkscrew curls.

But last night Julie had given her curls very like the ones in her dream. And this morning she was standing shivering outside the same house, as rejected and alone as she had been in her dream.

Alex clasped her arms round herself. 'Coincidence,' she

said aloud. But she had never believed in coincidence. And she didn't believe in dreams either.

In fact, now that she had thought about the dream, she remembered that when she had fled from the house, it was not to escape her grandmother's machinations, but something darker and stronger. Something that had nearly consumed her. Something that continued to pursue her even into the street. A man …more than a man . . .

In spite of not believing in dreams, Alex looked round to see if the man was following her as he had done in the dream last night. It was ridiculous, of course. She realised it at once. But she still could not suppress a little sigh of relief that the street remained deserted.

Alex put her hand to her cheek. The fingers were icy. The wind blew again.

This was ridiculous. She could not go on marching up and down outside the Eyre headquarters in a temper. She had to go back and deal with the situation. Just like she always did. Calm, sensible Alex, who would do the right thing, no matter how badly everyone else behaved.

'Tie a knot and go on,' she muttered ironically.

Raging but resigned, Alex went back into her office. With enforced calm, she sat down at her desk and looked at her email.

There were a number of messages. Lavender – well, of course. She did not read Lavender's messages and instead scrolled on down the list.

There was one from Rupert about a dinner party he wanted them both to go to. He knew Alex did not like the host, but it was a networking opportunity, he wrote. He really could not afford to miss it. This was his career, she would understand that, so he had accepted for both of them.

Alex sighed and made a note in her diary.

The other emails were all professional. Some were simply to say 'thank you' for the previous night's party. Most concerned business matters that had to be dealt with. Lavender could deal with those, thought Alex, forwarding them with satisfaction. Or she could try to get Caroline to sort them out. Fat chance of that!

And one was from Joe Gomez.

Arrested, Alex scanned it quickly. It was typically brief and enigmatic. They needed to talk, he said. She would see that. He had booked a table at *Serenata* for one, and hoped to see her there. If she couldn't make it, he'd be in touch.

Alex sat back in her chair. Her eyes narrowed to slits. Another message from Lavender bleeped onto the screen, but she ignored it. She was thinking.

chapter four

Joe did not really expect Alex to be there.

He knew he had shocked her last night – well, he had shocked himself, too. But Alex was not a woman you could easily get away with shocking. She liked life to go smoothly, and put a lot of effort into keeping it that way. Joe had a shrewd suspicion that the thing she would really hold against him was the way she had responded.

Well, there was only one way to find out.

He tried to phone her. When the assistant said she was in a meeting, some devil made him throw out that invitation to lunch, knowing it would probably infuriate her.

He should have asked the boys to give him their odds on the chances of her turning up, Joe thought wryly.

Anyway, there was more chance of getting her to lunch than to dinner. He did not think she would ever have dinner with him, not after the horrified way she had looked at him last night. If her expression was anything to go by, there was more chance of her accepting an invitation to a ball from Count Dracula himself. But lunch was different. It took place out of the dangerous dark. There were never any questions about where you went or what you did afterwards. He knew, after last night, that Alex would be very, very jumpy about 'afterwards'. And with lunch, the problem simply did not arise. You said a civilised goodbye, and then went back to work. She would find that reassuring.

So, Joe went to the fashionable Italian restaurant straight from his meeting, fully expecting to be eating on his own. He even had a briefcase full of papers to keep him company when she didn't turn up. Like he had said to Tom earlier, it never paid to run from the truth.

So he stopped dead when the first thing he saw as he walked in the restaurant was a dark, curly head bent in concentration over the menu.

'Your guest, Mr Gomez,' murmured the maître d'. 'I gave her a dry Martini and told her you must have been caught in traffic.'

Joe could not take his eyes off her. She was wearing one of her awful, ill-fitting tartan jackets and her hair was in her eyes. He thought he had never seen anything more beautiful in his life.

'Thanks, Mario,' he said absently. He thrust the briefcase at him. 'Lose that for me, will you?'

Alex looked up as he approached. It did not look as if the Martini had been touched. He saw that under her curtain of dark hair, she was very pale. He had meant to tell her to forget last night, that it had been a momentary aberration and wouldn't happen again. But it went right out of his head when he saw her expression.

'What's wrong?' he said involuntarily.

For a moment she looked startled, almost vulnerable.

Hell, what was he thinking about? *Almost* vulnerable? After last night, he knew exactly how vulnerable she was. He could not pretend anything else. She had kissed him like a woman who had found her heart's desire. But the moment she realised what she had done, she panicked. He was not going to forget the tears in her eyes easily. They were what made him realise he had ruined his chances with Alex Eyre.

Now, her dark lashes flickered. He was almost sure that she squared her shoulders as she spoke.

'I want to talk to you about that.'

Here it comes, Joe thought. She has made a policy decision that last night did not happen. This is where she tells me it meant nothing. And I'm never to touch her again.

He did not think he could bear it, for some reason. To forestall her, he said hastily, 'Hey, don't make a melodrama out of it.'

She blinked, as if he had startled her. Joe slipped into the seat opposite her.

'OK, I admit it. I was out of line last night. I was tempted. So I kissed you. I've never been any good at resisting temptation.'

Her eyes widened. They were wonderful eyes, brown as polished rosewood in firelight and flecked with gold. They made you feel warm just to look at them. Well, they were making him warm, anyway.

'No post-mortems, please. No apologies,' Joe said with determination. 'Hell, it was only a kiss after all.'

'Y-yes,' she said faintly. 'I mean...that wasn't what I wanted to talk about.'

'It wasn't?' He stared. 'But you said...'

'I said there was something wrong,' Alex answered steadily in her quiet voice. 'There is. But it's nothing to do with last night. It's...' Quite suddenly her voice seemed to give out.

Joe watched her jaw clench as she fought tears. He was bewildered. It made him feel helpless, and he didn't like it.

Alex fished in her pocket and brought out a rather grubby tissue. She blew her nose hard. 'Sorry about that,' she said, more steadily this time. 'I don't seem to be quite in control yet. Give me a moment.'

She took a sip of the Martini and blew her nose again, then sat back and met his eyes.

This time, there was no doubt, Joe observed. She had squared her shoulders visibly.

Joe's defensiveness fell away like a coat he had shrugged off. Her expression moved him. He leaned forward and covered her free hand with his own.

'Tell me. What has happened to upset you like this?'

Alex flushed slightly. 'My grandmother fired me,' she said baldly.

'*What?!*'

'I said, my grandmother fired me.'

Joe stared at her blankly. He would never have guessed that in a million years.

'Why on earth did she do that?'

Alex pressed her lips together. 'Family reasons.'

He shook his head. 'That's some crazy family you must have.'

Alex gave a ghost of a smile. 'We're not very…' she hesitated as she chose the word carefully '…united.'

'United! For your grandmother to do something so stupid, you would have to be sworn enemies.'

Alex did not smile. She looked away. 'Something like that.'

Joe realised suddenly that this was big. Alex had never told him anything about herself before. Everything he knew about her – and he knew a lot – had come from careful observation. He was not sure that she realised that she had just made the first, cautious step towards confiding in him now. But he knew. He felt as if he had been given a present.

Before she could recognise it and go into retreat, he said swiftly, 'Lavender must be out of her mind. The place will be in chaos within a week.'

His reward was an ironic, if slightly damp, smile.

'Thank you,' Alex said with real gratitude. 'I was beginning to wonder if I was letting vanity run away with me.'

'What vanity?' Joe asked dryly. 'You're the most self-effacing woman I've ever met.' He heard what he had said and stopped. 'Is *that* why? Lavender has never realised how much you do. Now someone has told her – or she's seen it for herself – so she's decided she can do without the competition! Only room for one Queen Bee in the hive?'

Alex gave him a real smile, wide and amused. It lit her eyes, still luminous from the threatened tears.

'Thank you, again. But it's not as simple as that.'

Her eyes are almost gold when she's sad, Joe thought,

astonished. *Like a dying bonfire with unsuspected heat still flickering up among the twigs.*

'What?' he said, distracted.

'I said, it's not so simple…' Alex broke off. 'What is it? Why are you staring at me like that?' She groaned suddenly. 'Oh no, don't tell me! Smudged lipstick, right?'

Joe wished she hadn't said that. It directed his attention to her mouth.

That mouth had always disturbed him. He had told her, too. 'Your mouth is too passionate, Alex,' he had said on that damned picnic. 'It will get you into trouble.' But she had only laughed, as if he'd said she had a smudge on her nose or something. And then she had gone off with Rupert Sweetcroft to look at some place in the woods where they had played together as children. Rupert Sweetcroft behaved as if he had not looked at her since she was a child, either. Joe thought it then, and had seen no reason to change his mind since. Rupert certainly didn't seem to have noticed that passionate mouth.

But Alex needed an answer. She was looking at him anxiously. Why did the woman have so little confidence? What did it matter if her lipstick smudged? thought Joe, irritated.

He cleared his throat and said curtly, 'Your lipstick is fine.'

'Are you sure?'

He pulled himself together. 'Positive. Why?'

'Because Lavender is always telling me that I make a mess of it.'

'Queen Bee,' said Joe again. 'Don't let it worry you. Now, tell me what you want to eat. And then tell me what you want me to do about this nonsense of you being fired.'

Alex blushed. 'What could you possibly do?'

'I've been asking myself that,' Joe said calmly. 'But the fact that you're here says you think I can do something. So just tell me what.'

Alex stared. 'You're very astute.'

He smiled at her then, a wide, open smile full of affection.

'Yup, that's me.'

Alex blinked at that beam of pleasure.

'Have I said something stupid?' she asked cautiously.

He shook his head. 'No, it's just that I haven't been called astute before. "Sharp operator" is usually more what the papers call me.'

'I *have* said something stupid.'

'No, of course you haven't. Anyway, given the choice, I prefer "astute". Has a ring to it. Sounds more substantial.'

Alex was beginning to feel alarmed. 'Why would you want to sound more substantial?'

Joe grinned. 'As far as European architects are concerned, I'm a Johnny-come-lately. And about twenty years too young. My press tends to emphasise that. Along with the fast cars and the Hollywood mansions. But it's all media hype. I'm an OK guy, really. You can trust me.'

He did not *look* very trustworthy, Alex thought, suddenly. He looked like a pirate. For a moment, she almost abandoned her idea.

But then Joe said, 'If you dare, of course.'

She sat bolt upright and narrowed her eyes at him.

'Are you calling me a coward?'

He looked amused. 'Would I? A little cautious, maybe.'

'Cautious!'

The problem was that it was true. So true that Alex lost her temper. She lost her normal common sense along with it.

She said with sudden fury, 'You've been pestering me to work for you for weeks. Do you want to wriggle out of it now?'

'Months,' he murmured.

She was put out. 'What?'

'Months. I've been pestering you for months. Ever since I saw you at that board meeting,' he reminded her helpfully.

That was the time he had stood in the doorway and said raptly, 'I'm in love.' Alex did not need reminding. She glared.

'Tell me why.'

'Why?' He put his mind to explaining it. 'Because I can't run the place myself and do all the schmoozing too. To say nothing of the creative stuff, which is why I became an architect in the first place. Because nobody I get in seems to be any better at it. Because the more successful we are, the closer we get to the brink of complete chaos. Because I'm going mad.'

'You must have someone doing the day-to-day admin at the moment.'

'We have,' he said gloomily.

'And?'

'She can't keep her butt on the seat for longer than ten minutes together. And so far she has lost six files, every single contact address between D and H, and a scale model of an arts complex.'

Alex gave a choke, which she rapidly turned into a cough. Then she cleared her throat and said, 'OK.'

She did not say anything else, though Joe waited.

Eventually he said, 'I think I missed a couple of steps. "OK", what?'

'OK, I'll run your office for you,' Alex said baldly – and not very graciously.

Joe stared at her as if he had been turned to stone.

Alex shifted uncomfortably. If she was honest – and Alex was usually honest with *herself* – she had to acknowledge that she did not sound like the ideal employee. Instead, she sounded like a truculent schoolgirl, which was going to make the next bit even harder to sell.

'There's a price.'

Joe came out of his statue-imitation mode. 'Oh?'

'Yes. No more "good old Alex, you don't have to worry about a contract, we'll shake hands on a deal",' she said bitterly. 'I want equity.'

Joe snapped to attention. 'You want *what*?'

'Equity. I want to be a full partner. I want some control over my life. I don't want to go on the payroll and then find myself slung off when you get a better idea.'

'But…a partner!'

'I'll put money into the business, of course.'

Joe frowned. 'I'll give you a contract, of course. A contract of employment. But partnership is a big step.'

'Quite,' said Alex tersely. 'If I join you, I want to be sure you're really committed to the idea.'

Joe was silent. 'And what about you? If I'm committed, so are you.'

Alex showed her teeth. 'That's all right. I'm good at commitment. My family may be rotten, but I'm not. When I promise to do something, I stick at it.'

She thought he would smile, but he didn't. He frowned grimly, like a pirate weighing the risk of battle against the chance of treasure.

She leaned forward and said urgently, 'You said you needed me. Don't you?'

His eyes lifted. She had the impression that he was thinking something very dark and complicated, and that it made him angry.

But all he said was, 'I need you.' There was no emotion in his voice at all.

There was an odd little silence. Alex sat back, not sure whether she had won or lost the point. 'Well then,' she said uncertainly.

Joe shifted. 'Tell you what I'll do,' he said. 'You come and work for me for three months. Proper contract, proper salary and we'll think about some equity options. We can talk about partnership in the New Year if it all works out. If it doesn't – or you want to go back and work for Lavender anyway – then we can say goodbye. No hard feelings. No complicated dissolving of partnership agreements. What do you say?'

Suddenly, he was the man she knew again – not a pirate,

but a sunny negotiator, the relaxed guy who always got people to see his side of things in the end.

Alex was a lot more disappointed than she wanted to admit. 'Now who's a coward?' she jeered.

He shrugged, not denying it. 'I'm not going into partnership with anyone on the spur of the moment like that. I'm not even sure that's what you really want.'

'I…'

He held up a hand. 'You're mad at your grandmother. Quite right, too. But that's no basis for you and me getting together.'

Alex was bewildered. 'But I thought you wanted to.' She felt ruffled and inclined to be indignant.

'So did I,' said Joe ruefully. 'Just not like this.'

She looked at the tablecloth and balked. 'You only wanted me when you thought you couldn't have me,' she said bitterly. 'Story of my life.'

His eyes narrowed alertly, but Alex did not see it. She was too busy turning and turning the full Martini glass.

After a moment, Joe said, 'I think you need to go and talk this through with someone.'

She looked up and opened her mouth.

He read her expression, and flung up a hand. '*Not* me. I'm an interested party. Haven't you got anyone else you can ask advice from? What about your father?'

Alex shook her head violently. 'Bad idea.'

'Why?'

'Family feud,' she said briefly. 'I can't ask Dad about anything that involves mother or Lavender. And vice versa.'

'Why the hell not?'

She struggled to explain. 'It's a sort of code I put together for myself when they broke up. Well, before, really. I don't take sides. And I don't tell either side anything that the other could use against them, if you see what I mean.'

'So who do you ask for advice?'

'When one of the parents is involved, I don't usually,' said

Alex. 'I just try to work it out for myself.'

He looked appalled. 'What, always? Sounds very lonely.'

She thought about it. 'Sometimes I talk stuff through with the friend I share my house with.'

Joe looked relieved. He had met Julie when Lavender held a picnic at Hope House in the summer. He obviously approved of her, thought Alex. But then, men usually did approve of the gorgeous Julie. Alex found she was not entirely pleased at this, and berated herself for being catty. However, this was because she was feeling betrayed by Lavender. The shock of her grandmother's treachery had not yet worn off. Alex had never really resented Julie's popularity. Or at least, she never had before. So why should she care if Joe Gomez fancied Julie rotten?

She said, almost to herself, 'The moment you start to feel sour about something, the nastiness spreads all around, doesn't it?'

'Exactly my point,' said Joe.

Alex sighed. 'I suppose so.' She felt tired and a bit weepy, now that her grand design had collapsed.

He gave her a look of considerable understanding.

'You need to take yourself for a walk round the block and kick a few grandmother substitutes,' he said shrewdly. 'If you still want to come work for me after that, we can sort something out. I'll talk to my lawyer, get him to draw up a contract. You talk this over with Julie…'

So he not only approved of her, he remembered her name from three months ago, thought Alex, with a little stab of something that could almost be envy. Except that she was never envious on principle, and Julie was her friend.

'…And we'll speak again tomorrow morning,' Joe continued, unaware of Alex's internal struggles. 'And you'd better come over and see the place, just to make sure you know what you're taking on. You've got my numbers?'

Alex could not remember. She shook her head 'No'.

He fished a business card out of his top pocket and passed it across the table.

'And yours?'

She told him. He produced a platinum pen and scribbled it down on the back of another of his own cards.

'Fine.' He capped the pen and stowed her telephone number carefully in his breast pocket. 'Now, forget the whole thing and let me spoil you. Do you like caviar?'

'Spoil me?' Alex asked in an odd voice.

'You sound as if no one has ever done it before,' he said, amused.

She was suddenly flushed and looking awkward.

'Well, not for a long time.'

'Fine. The trick is, you tell me all your favourite things – and I filter them back to you as surprises over time.'

She laughed suddenly. He watched with pleasure. That wicked little curl of the tempestuous mouth, what a pleasure it was to have made it tremble like that!

Careful, Gomez, he thought with wry self-mockery. *You're feeling warm again. Calm down. Treat this one with kid gloves, or she'll run.*

But she wasn't running yet. She was sitting on the other side of the table, teasing him right back.

'Starting with caviar?'

'Whatever turns you on,' said Joe with irony.

Alex did not notice. 'What really turns me on…' she sighed wistfully.

Joe Gomez, master flirt of the western world, felt his heart beat faster.

'Yes?'

'It's impossible, I know,' she murmured.

He leaned forward. 'Nothing is impossible.

'Well then…' She looked up at him, all wide, appealing eyes and spaniel hair. 'It's marmalade sandwiches.'

He blinked, completely taken aback.

She flung back her head and laughed, peal after peal of golden relish.

After a moment, Joe laughed too. As a piece of retaliatory mockery, it was perfect. He had not seen it coming. And now it had come, there was not a thing he could do to get her what she claimed to want. Not in one of the best restaurants in the capital.

He said wryly, 'You've got me there.'

She bit her tongue at him like a gamine.

'Good.' Alex was purring.

'But for future reference,' he prompted. 'What else would go on the spoiling list? Apart from marmalade sandwiches, that is.'

'Food and drink?'

'Anything.'

'Anything. Gosh.' She considered. 'Well, I like flowers. Garden ones mostly. Things that smell nice. Wallflowers and lilac and jasmine.'

Joe looked at her with deep suspicion. 'Is this a test?'

She widened her eyes innocently. 'Test? Why?'

'You know perfectly well they're all things I can't send you. No florist stocks them.'

'But you have sent me wonderful bouquets all this year. You really don't need to send me any more.'

He realised suddenly that his Alex was better at this teasing flirtation than he would ever have believed possible. He sat back, grinning.

'OK. I have to pick the flowers myself. Got that. What else? Do I have to make the chocolates?'

'I don't like chocolate,' Alex said cheerfully.

'You're a difficult woman.'

Her laughter bubbled over.

'All right. I like real lace handkerchiefs, pottery mugs with elephants on them and any good red wine. Will that do?'

Joe shook his head. 'Shifty. Not precise enough. What

colour elephants? And how do I know you will think the wine is good?'

She smiled, not with her mouth, her eyes. And she smiled right into his.

'The elephants,' she said composedly, 'should be grey. And the wine should taste of a hot summer afternoon in the fields.'

He reached for her hand, his eyes not leaving hers.

'Got it,' he said softly.

He turned the hand over and carried her palm to his lips. And saw, as he looked into those laughing, golden-brown depths, the convulsive shiver she could not disguise.

'I look on this,' he said, 'as a challenge.'

And he was not talking about her wish list.

Alex did not mention the idea to Julie. She did not want to hear her flatmate raving about Joe Gomez for some reason. And on the principle of playing absolutely fair by her family, she did not mention it to any of them. That included Rupert.

She did, however, call her solicitor.

'It sounds as if he's trying to play fair by you,' he said. 'Let me have a look at the contract when he sends it over, though. And don't sign any cheques.'

'Listen, he hasn't asked me for money. I'm the one who wants to buy in.'

'Forget it,' said her solicitor kindly. 'For one thing, you don't have the qualifications. For another, he is very, very successful. You might have some trouble raising the ante. Unless you want to go to the Trust, of course.'

Asking her trustees for capital meant letting Lavender know her business. Alex said forcefully that she didn't want to do that.

'Then resign yourself to being an employee.'

She did. But Joe had a better idea.

'I don't know how you feel about it,' he said, on the phone the next morning. 'It's a risk. And it wouldn't be full-time.

Most of the time, you'd be working for the partnership. But it would give you a stake. You might even have a bit of fun as well.'

He gave her a potted account of Tom Skelton, natural justice and the popular appetite for architectural knowledge.

'A television series?' said Alex doubtfully. 'What would I have to do?'

'Trouble-shoot the admin. All the technical stuff is Tom's bag. All the subject matter of the programme is mine. You keep the bills paid and the schedule on track. Can you do it?'

'Yes,' said Alex, who knew she could after many turbulent years of taking her grandmother's company global.

'Then think about it. But come and see us, anyway. This afternoon? Three o' clock?'

That gave him time to talk the younger architects into accepting her, though at first they were not very enthusiastic.

'Cosmetics?' Charlie said doubtfully. 'Not a lot of synergy with architecture, there.'

Joe shrugged. 'Office systems are office systems.'

'Alexandra Eyre?' said one of the others. He was well connected, but Joe had taken him on in spite of it. 'My sister used to go to school with her. Doesn't say boo to a goose. And she's terribly stiff.'

They looked depressed. Gomez and Partners was too small to house any difficult temperaments. Someone prickly and silent could blow the whole relaxed atmosphere for everyone.

Joe took swift action. 'Look, she's the answer to our prayers. An efficient, experienced, conscientious answer. OK, maybe she can be a bit stiff sometimes. Maybe she's shy. Anyway, what does it matter? We're falling apart here. We need someone to run this office, not a limbo dancer.'

They all shuffled, unconvinced.

Joe thought of Alex sticking her tongue out at him at the

restaurant. He grinned. They would find out their mistake in time. Meanwhile…

'If it's limbo dancing you want, Peta is your woman. Those legs must have been forty-five inches long. Along with the six-inch fingernails, she would have been phenomenal. Do you want to stick with her?'

There was resounding denial.

'OK, then. Alex it is. Let's just hope I can get her to agree.'

Charlie raised his head, alertly.

Joe did not notice. 'Alex Eyre, I need you,' he said aloud, experimenting.

Charlie looked at his watch and made a note.

So, in the end, three things happened that day to change Alex's life forever.

First, the Managing Director of Eyre Associates rang from Singapore, begging her to tell him that she had not left.

'Sorry, Gerald. Lavender has sacked me. I'm gone,' said Alex, aware of burning her boats. 'Good luck.' He almost sobbed.

The second milestone was when she signed the agreement and became a shareholder in Sage Productions.

And the third, though it took her some time to realise just how significant this change would turn out to be, was when Charlie came into the office she was to share with Joe, bearing a magnum of champagne and followed by the rest of the team.

He plonked the bottle down in front of Joe and produced plastic cups.

'Open it, boss. You did it.'

'Did what?' said Alex suspiciously.

'Well, you described her as "professional to her toes",' Charlie reminded Joe. 'And you managed to grab her for the Company.' He turned to the others. 'Pay out on four weeks,' he announced.

'Pay out?' queried Alex.

Charlie gave her a naughty grin. 'The wager run by the office. That was the shortest time anyone gave him. Most of us thought it would take months. But Joe always beats the odds.' He held out his hand and shook hers vigorously. 'Welcome to the Funfair, Alex.'

chapter five

'Funfair' just about covered it. Alex had never imagined any place of work could be so much fun.

For one thing, it was completely relaxed. When he was not dressed in his city suits and silk-lined waistcoats, Joe wandered around in cut-off sailor's pants. The others were just the same, wearing whatever they felt like. Jeans were positively formal. No one wore a tie. Hell, when he was working on a model, Joe did not even wear a shirt.

Alex developed the habit of swallowing hard and getting on with her work. It was not easy, for all sorts of reasons. Of course, it was disconcerting to find a wild-eyed workman with wood shavings in his hair padding around her neat work environment. But it was the flexing muscles that really made her blink. She was not used to being around men who routinely stripped off to square up to the task in hand.

'This never happened at Eyre Associates,' she remarked one day, picking her way around Joe as he lay spread-eagled on the floor peering along the sight line of a modelled embankment.

He turned and grinned up at her. With his khaki singlet and bare feet, he looked as if he was just about to swing into jungle action, Alex thought.

'All that's missing is the machete between your teeth,' she said involuntarily.

He laughed aloud. 'See what you've been missing all these years! Time to live a little.'

'Thank you,' said Alex sedately.

But her quiet manner could not hide her enjoyment. She had never had so much fun in her life.

That did not mean it was easy. Joe was demanding, intelligent and inspirational, but his best friend would not say he was organised. And when he wanted to do something, he was impatient with all the obstacles. That included staying solvent, as Alex found when the television project began to take shape.

'This thing will never get out of the red,' she told him. 'We haven't got enough pre-sales.'

'Don't worry,' said Joe airily. 'When people see how good it is, they'll be queuing up to buy it.'

'And they'll get it at a garage-sale price, unless we smarten our ideas up,' said Alex sharply. She turned to Tom. 'What about that Japanese education network? Have you talked to them again?'

Tom looked at Joe for advice. 'We …er …I …thought we didn't need to. Once we'd got the UK sorted.'

Alex sighed. 'We haven't got the UK sorted. We've got some cautious interest. You can't bank cautious interest. No filming until somebody signs.'

It was the start of her first office fight with Joe. He went nuclear.

'You have no vision,' he yelled at her.

And Alex, who had hated loud voices all her life, yelled right back, 'You don't pay me for vision. You pay me to keep us afloat. That's what I'm doing.'

There was a simmering pause. Then Joe subsided, pushing his hand through his riotously disordered hair.

'You're right,' he said at last, ruefully. 'You always are. That's a real irritating habit you've got there.'

Alex beamed.

His assistants learned that if you wanted Joe to see sense, it paid to have Alex on your side. She became the hub of the practice. It was, she often thought, like having suddenly acquired a family of brothers. Heady stuff for a woman who had never really known what it was to be a child.

They seemed to fight all the time. Huge battles blew up from nowhere like tropical storms, and died away just as fast. Usually, Alex discovered, because one of the combatants made the others laugh. For the first time in her life, she heard raised voices and did not want to run for cover.

Once, she told Joe shyly about this.

He was thoughtful. 'You're a natural peacemaker, my love. That's a good thing, but you can take it too far. Sometimes people need to clear the air.'

'Yes,' said Alex, randomly.

He had taken to calling her 'my love' in gentle teasing, after he had found her reading an historical novel. He had picked it up, and one of the paragraphs had appealed to his wayward sense of humour.

'*The gentlemen, my love, must never be contradicted. It puts them out,*' he read aloud and laughed immoderately. 'That's good advice, Alex. Hang onto it, *my love.*'

Of course, it was not in the least bit sexual. The speaker in the book was an aunt speaking to her niece, and Joe, who knew every form of innuendo there was, never used the phrase in any other tone than gentle mockery.

But every time he called her his 'love' like that, the hair came up on the back of Alex's neck and she had trouble breathing. Fortunately, nobody seemed to notice.

Around all the fun, she managed to introduce a logging system for incoming work, which meant that the new office assistant could keep track of progress. Fran, the new assistant, was a trainee architect taking a year out to earn some money, and was really over-qualified. But she liked the idea of doing research on the television project, Joe liked her resourceful approach to life and Charlie liked her clubbing expertise. She became part of the team in a matter of hours.

'You're brilliant,' Joe told Alex. 'None of the other trainees ever settled in.'

'It's all a question of giving them a decent job description.

If they know what you want, they can do it. You just can't expect them to sort out stuff they don't understand.'

'And you can,' he said, ruffling her hair. 'Like I said – brilliant.'

Alex began to feel as if she was doing a good job – everyone told her so, anyway – and she blossomed. She did not just set up office systems, either. She picked up every job that nobody else saw coming, from crisis plumbing to writing speeches for Joe, who'd forgotten that he was the keynote speaker at a dinner he was going to one night. She spent about a day a week on the television project; she nursed architectural clients; she sweet-talked suppliers; she learned about virtual construction on some terrifyingly advanced software; and she found there was nothing she could not do if she kept her wits about her. In fact, Alex felt as if her feet never touched the ground.

That was just as well, as every time she stopped to take stock, her family told her what a mistake she was making.

'The fellow's a con man,' said her father. 'I wouldn't want Laine to get involved with him.' A thought occurred to him and he had added sharply, 'I hope you haven't put any money into that business of his.'

Alex returned an evasive answer and escaped from the fashionable cocktail lounge as soon as she could. She had avoided going down to her father and stepmother's house on the plea of having too much work, but she knew that she could not put it off forever. Laine's dance loomed on the horizon. She tried not to think about it. Arguing about Joe was a good way of distracting her father from that particular hot potato.

'Joe Gomez is just using you,' said her mother, tapping her frenetic way around a private view at an art gallery. 'Be realistic,' she added in an urgent undertone. 'Come back to Lavender. There's no future for you with Joe Gomez.'

In spite of herself, Alex was intrigued. 'Are you so sure?'

'Yes,' said Caroline. 'He's going to be a world name in the next couple of years. See how fast he'll unload you then.'

'Thank you, Mother,' said Alex with irony as the older woman accepted a glass of champagne from a waiter like it was water in the desert. She drank half a glass in one sip.

'You wait and see,' Caroline said with energy.

'All right,' said Alex equably. 'Now, why don't we go and get some food? You know you don't like these pictures, and my feet are killing me.'

Her mother drained the glass first. But she did at least start moving, which was more than she did when Lavender set her a task.

Lavender, realising her mistake with every day that passed and shouted at regularly by her managing director, finally unbent enough to call her granddaughter.

'I think your mother could do with some help easing into the job,' she said airily, quite as if she had never told Alex to go round the world for a year and get out of her mother's limelight. 'Let's talk.'

'Let's not,' said Alex, pleasant but firm. 'My career has taken a new turn.'

But Lavender, all dignified affront, had an even more unflattering take on the situation than anyone else. She cornered Alex at a cocktail party given by Diana Holding and gave a tinkling laugh.

'Oh really, Alex. You should know better.'

'What do you mean?' said Alex warily.

She knew Lavender. She had not become an international businesswoman by chance. She had developed the skill of manipulating others into an art form.

Now she said cosily, 'The thing about Joe Gomez is that he can't bear to be beaten. All men are the same, darling. But Joe's got it in spades. Men of that class so often have. You haven't got a new career, you've got a walk-on part.'

Alex kept her tone neutral. 'Oh?'

Lavender's voice sharpened. 'As soon as he wins, he'll lose interest. I'm sorry to say it, but there it is.'

'Wins what?' said Alex, torn between amusement and simple curiosity.

Lavender widened her enormous blue eyes. 'The battle, of course.'

'What battle?' said Alex with patience.

'I challenged him,' said Lavender superbly.

Alex blinked. '*You* challenged him?'

'I said that he couldn't get you to work for him. So, he just couldn't resist.'

Alex was speechless. Lavender gave her a nicely judged smile, in which grandmotherly concern mingled with superior sophistication.

'You don't think it could be anything to do with me?' Alex suggested when she could speak. 'Like, he saw that I was good at what I do, and thought his business could do with some of my magic?'

The faintest frown creased Lavender's perfect brow.

'Don't be silly, darling. Of course, you're a good little worker. But you don't do magic. You're not *creative*. No, Joe and I have been locked in a duel ever since I turned down his plan for the cellars at Hope Place, I'm afraid. You just happen to be his choice of weapon.'

Alex laughed aloud.

Lavender raised haughty eyebrows.

'Good try, Grandma,' said Alex affectionately. 'No sale.'

Lavender stiffened.

'You wanted to give the job to Mother. So you did. Live with it,' she advised. 'I'm on a new road. And I'm having fun.'

She was, too. And the most startling thing of all was that Rupert seemed to resent it.

At first, Alex did not believe it. But Rupert had moved

rapidly from disapproval at the news of the partnership to cold fury whenever Joe's name was mentioned.

'Can it be this man is jealous?' murmured Julie, after one icy exchange over the communal breakfast table.

The front door banged behind Rupert, echoing through the house.

Alex had turned away to hide tears. The downside of loving someone since you were six, she sometimes thought, was that you never got out of the six-year-old's vulnerability. Rupert could still make her cry. All it took was a cold glance, and she was back in a lonely place, chilled and small and disappearing.

But at that she turned round to face Julie again, bewildered. 'Why should he be? He's got a perfectly good career of his own.'

Julie gave an exaggerated sigh. 'Not of the career. Of Joe.'

Joe was becoming an increasingly familiar visitor at the house. Julie adored him. The two of them talked as easily as if they had known each other all their lives. Alex supposed that it was a natural affinity. They certainly spoke the same language.

Now she looked at Julie as if she was speaking ancient Greek. 'Why should he be jealous of Joe?'

Julie cast her eyes to the ceiling gave an exaggerated sigh. 'Because Joe is to die for. He looks like a pirate, and then he goes and purrs at you like a jaguar. Every right-thinking woman drools at the sight of him.'

'I don't,' objected Alex, laughing. And she didn't. Well, not quite. But she was startled.

'I said *right-thinking* woman.' Julie half closed her eyes and rocked on the stool, contemplating Joe's attractions. 'When you talk to him he listens – *really* listens,' she said dreamily. 'You get all his attention. Have you seen the way his eyes go black when he's concentrating?' She gave a little shiver of pleasurable alarm. 'Delicious. But scary. I'll bet he's a red-hot lover. I bet he would . . .'

'Stop right there,' Alex said resolutely, knowing Julie. 'I have to work with the man. I don't want to have to remember your fantasies about his sexual technique every time I look at him.'

Julie gave her a bland smile. 'The hell with my fantasies. What about yours?'

Alex shook her head. 'I don't have sexual fantasies about men I work with,' she said firmly. 'Point of principle. It's the kiss of death to a professional relationship.'

Julie gave a little wriggle. 'Kiss,' she murmured, lingering on the word as if she could taste it. 'Mmm, yes, *nice!*'

Alex threw a croissant at her. 'You're a nymphomaniac,' she said, exasperated. 'With a horrible sense of humour.'

Julie laughed and gave up. 'OK, you can't see that Joe Gomez is red hot. But believe me, Rupert sees it. That's what's getting on his wick.'

But that was not what Rupert said. *Rupert* said that he was concerned about Alex. 'You are making a fool of yourself,' he said icily two days later.

They were taking one of his out-of-town clients to dinner. He had called for Alex before going on to the visitors' hotel to pick them up. The moment they got into the taxi, the words had burst out.

Alex thought: he's been rehearsing this. That's not like Rupert. He usually just says what he wants as soon as he thinks of it. What's this about?

'A complete fool. Everyone says so.'

'What are you talking about?'

'Joining up with that – that *playboy.*'

Alex's sense of justice stirred. 'Joe is not a playboy,' she protested. 'He works extremely hard.'

In the uncertain light of the taxi, Rupert looked at her with an expression that shocked her. It seemed almost to border on dislike. Alex shrank back into her corner, feeling the old chill strike at her heart.

Rupert did not notice. 'Sometimes I wonder if you really are naïve,' he said with controlled fury, 'or if you just say things like that to annoy people. I meant he screws around. Is that plain enough for you?'

His tone, as much as his words, made it sound ugly.

Alex flinched, but she said levelly, 'What has that got to do with me?'

Rupert closed his eyes and muttered something. She did not want to ask him to repeat it. He opened his eyes.

'You're rich,' he said, as if he was explaining arithmetic to a three-year-old. 'You're no glamour girl. You've lost your way. Your job was important to you, and Lavender kicked you out. So you're looking for something. Joe Gomez is a gypsy, but he might just provide it.'

Alex felt the blood drain out of her cheeks. Rupert could not see it, of course, in the reflected streetlights, but he must have sensed something of her reaction. He appeared a little conscience-stricken.

'I know it's nothing like that, of course,' he said hastily. 'But that's what everyone will say.'

Alex rallied. 'I think you must be mistaken. I mean I…'

Something snapped in Rupert. He shouted, 'It's what they are saying already. Like *now*, Alex.'

The taxi driver turned his head a little.

This time Alex went bright red. She felt her cheeks burn with it.

'Then they're very stupid,' she flashed. 'And so are you to take any notice. I'm not going to let it bother me.'

And from that position, she would not be moved.

It was Rupert's turn for incredulity. He had never imagined such a thing. Alex – peaceable, easy-going Alex – never stuck her chin in the air and told the world to do its worst. She had certainly never defied *him*. Since he was ten, all he had ever had to do was express a faint preference, and Alex jumped to oblige. Now, here she was telling him categorically that his wishes did not count. She wanted to work with Joe Gomez, and she was quite determined to carry on doing so. Rupert could like it or lump it.

Rupert was reduced to pleading. He was not used to it, and he did not do it well. 'You might think about my position,' he said sullenly. 'It makes me look such a fool.'

And peaceable, easy-going, *devoted* Alex, said, 'Tough.'

It did not end the argument, of course. That did not finish until they reached the hotel and collected their guests. And even then, it did not so much end as break off.

Rupert instituted a campaign of silent reproach. He was cool for the rest of the evening. He did not kiss her when he took her home, let alone suggest staying the night. Thereafter, he telephoned less frequently. He only took her out when they were with a group of friends.

When she showed no sign of seeing sense – or even of noticing that she was being punished – Rupert came round on a Sunday afternoon to announce that he was not going to be able to spend the night with her for the next couple of weeks.

He waited for Alex to protest.

But she only said ruefully, 'You too, huh? I'm really sorry about this, Rupert, but I think you're right. I'm just so *busy*. I'll make it up to you after Christmas, I promise.'

He was outraged.

He said, 'Be careful, Alex.' And when she stared at him, not understanding, he said in a goaded voice, 'Don't throw away something real for a mirage.'

And banged out of the house.

'What was that about?' asked Julie, emerging from the bathroom with her hair swirled up in a towel and her face covered in green goo.

Alex sat down rather hard. She felt oddly breathless, as if Rupert's throwaway exit line had hit the target somehow.

Not her heart, never her heart, of course. Her heart was Rupert's, and always would be. Nothing he could say could change that. But she still felt as if something had happened, as if the hawser that tethered her world in place had suffered major damage.

She did not know what. Or how. Or *why*. But she suddenly felt as if all the firm ground under her feet had started to sway uncertainly.

Julie perched on the window seat. 'Rupert not pleased with you?'

'It seems not,' said Alex, still distracted.

A *mirage?* What mirage? And what was she in danger of throwing away? Why did she suddenly feel so uncertain? Even threatened? Even *seasick*, for Heaven's sake!

'I take it this is about Joe.'

Alex pulled herself together. 'Everything in the whole world is about Joe,' she said bitterly.

Julie smiled like a cat that had got the cream. 'Told you so.'

'No you didn't,' retorted Alex. 'You said Rupert was jealous of him. You didn't say every damned member of my family would line up to slag him off.'

Even Julie was surprised. 'Really?' she said, intrigued.

'They all hate him.' Alex's innate fairness took over. 'Well, no, Lavender doesn't hate him. But she doesn't think I should have anything to do with him, either.' She ground her teeth in frustration. 'They only agree on one thing. He's too attractive to work with.'

'Hell, he's too attractive to *live*,' said Julie, unsurprised.

'But that's nothing to do with me. I just work with him,' said Alex with emphasis.

'Oh, sure.' Julie was patently unconvinced. 'So, what's he like to work for – I mean, with?'

'A whirlwind.' Alex thought about it. 'An opinionated whirlwind.'

Julie grinned. Her voice sank to a thrilling whisper, like the voiceover for a movie trailer that she had just done. 'How long before he blows the girl off her feet?'

Alex narrowed her eyes at Julie. The world seemed dangerously close to going into full-wave motion and taking her sea legs with it.

'If you think you're funny, I'm telling you that you're not,' she said coldly. 'As far as I'm concerned, Joe is a professional colleague.'

'Doesn't mean he isn't the last of the red-hot lovers,' Julie pointed out with justice. Her eyes gleamed. 'He's got the mouth for it.'

Alex suppressed the urge to agree with her. She gave an exaggerated sigh. 'You may not understand this, you green-faced sexpot, but to me, that means he's off-limits.'

'Oh yeah?'

'Yeah.' Alex was exasperated. 'Joe Gomez may well be the last of the red-hot lovers, and with rosettes to prove it. Wouldn't make my heart skip a beat. That's not how I think of him.'

Julie shook her head. 'Who's talking about thinking?'

'I am. That's what I do. I *think*.' Alex was nearly shouting. 'And I can't afford to think of the man I work for as a sex object. All right? Have you got the message? Am I making myself clear here?'

Julie blinked. 'Got it, flower. Whatever you say.'

Then, two weeks before Christmas, Alex's world did a back flip and turned upside-down.

To begin with, Alex thought it was because they were so busy. Joe had a diary full of site meetings and planning hearings but, every moment he could, he disappeared off with Tom to talk about the television project. Clients were beginning to complain. It took all her diplomacy to keep them on board.

Then, one Monday evening, she said as much to Joe.

He turned and looked at her. For a moment she thought he was going to explode.

'What is it?' Alex said involuntarily.

'Who do you think I am?' he snarled. 'Superman?'

'No, I don't. That's the whole point.' She tapped the diary. 'You can't go on like this.' She gave him her best professional smile, tolerant but firm. Or that's what she meant to do.

That's not how Joe took it. 'You know, you're really unbearable when you go into kindergarten-teacher mode,' he said conversationally. And did something he had not done, since the night she had all but wiped out of her memory: he kissed her, hard.

After a number of weeks at the Funfair, though, Alex was much better equipped to handle it.

'Get off!' she yelled, overbalancing.

Joe lifted his head and returned her to the upright position, his good humour restored.

Alex smoothed her hair with an unsteady hand.

'That's the second time you've done that,' she said heatedly.

He looked amused. 'I'm glad you remember.'

'*Remember?*'

'No one would guess.'

'Because I try to be professional...' Alex began stiffly.

But Joe interrupted her. 'You don't try to be professional. You try to be a robot. Damn near bring it off, too. What is it with you?'

Her mouth was still throbbing. Not unpleasantly, but she had to fight an urge to touch her fingertips to her lower lip. Her chin came up.

'But that's what you love about me,' she pointed out sweetly.

Joe stared. 'What are you talking about?'

'You fell in love with me when I was in kindergarten-teacher mode,' she retorted. 'I was bringing the Board to order during the row about the annual report, as I remember.'

His eyes narrowed. 'Oh you remember that too, do you?'

'Naturally. You stood there staring. Then you said, "I'm in love". It was very embarrassing.'

He flushed faintly. Alex was glad to see it.

'Yes, well…'

'What's more, that's why you persuaded me to come and work with you. And you know it. You *need* me to be a robot,' she finished triumphantly.

Joe's dark face was unreadable. 'You've got a real selective memory.'

'Salient facts only,' said Alex smugly.

'You have an odd idea of what is – what did you call it? – salient?'

'Salient,' she agreed. 'Anything that might affect the success of our business.'

He leaned against the bookshelf, as if he expected their exchange to go on all night. He folded his arms and scanned her face with laser intensity.

'Anything?' He sounded curious.

Alex nodded vigorously. 'Absolutely. Quality control. Delivery dates. Efficiency. Style. Reputation. The works.'

Joe mulled it over. 'What do you mean by reputation, exactly?'

Alex could answer that without stopping to think. She did. A bit of a mistake, as it turned out.

'Financial soundness. Honest contracts. Good working practices, that sort of thing,' she explained airily.

Joe's teeth gleamed very white in his dark face. 'And is it a good working practice to treat my right-hand person as a robot? Doesn't seem very respectful to me.'

'Ouch,' said Alex, realising too late that she had walked into her own trap. She made haste to repair the damage. 'It's just fine if I *want* to be treated as a robot,' she assured him.

One eyebrow rose. 'And do you?'

'Yes,' she said, with more fervour than was strictly necessary.

Joe seemed puzzled. 'Why?'

The repair was not holding.

'Because…because…' She was floundering. An unexpected flash of memory came to her aid. 'Because otherwise people will talk.'

He had not moved. He was still leaning against the bookshelf, looking sinfully handsome and amused, damn him. But she had the impression that it stopped him dead in his tracks.

'And that's important,' he said, as if he was agreeing with her. She had the impression that he was very angry all of a sudden.

'Well no, not important exactly,' said Alex uneasily. 'But it's easier if we don't give people any reason to think you and I…I mean, I wouldn't want anyone to get the wrong idea…to think that we…'

'Are lovers,' Joe supplied softly.

There was a terrible silence. Alex gulped. Joe said nothing, waiting for her to speak. His eyes were so dark they were quite unreadable. They were fixed unwaveringly on her face. Her hot face, Alex realised.

'Er …yes,' she said, at last. Much, much too late.

'Why not?' he asked vaguely, as if he did not much care, but found the subject mildly intriguing.

Alex could feel her face heating up the surrounding air. She took care not to meet his eyes.

'Lots of reasons.' She tried to sound airy, but merely ended up sounding breathless.

'Name one.'

And when she did not answer immediately, he said, 'Go on. I dare you.'

He was enjoying himself. He did not even try to disguise it. Sheer indignation made Alex pull herself together.

'Rupert!' she gasped.

Quite suddenly, she knew that Joe had stopped enjoying himself. Well, that was something, at least. Her shoulders sagged in relief.

He snapped his fingers. 'Oh, of course. Rupert. Sure. He'd sort of slipped out of my mind. I wonder why?'

Alex prudently did not answer that.

Joe pushed himself away from the bookshelf at last. She could not help herself. She jumped.

His eyes lifted swiftly to hers.

Damn! thought Alex, meeting that burning darkness. *That's torn it.* She did not have the slightest idea why.

She was suddenly aware that they were all alone in the building.

And then it all came tumbling back, just when she didn't want it to. That first kiss in Lavender's room. The dark, shadowed room. The heat of his body. His hunger. Her own. And then his withdrawal.

She gabbled, 'Rupert says that people are laughing at me because I'm a soppy spinster and you're a...a...' She shuddered to a halt, unable to find a neutral description for what Rupert thought Joe was.

Joe smiled. Not a nice smile. 'I can imagine.'

'Rupert says...'

Joe, she found, was suddenly in front of her, and much too close. His body was just as hot as she remembered. Hotter. But this time, he was not hungry. He was *furious.*

'You will not,' he said between his teeth, 'tell me what Rupert Sweetcroft says about you. Ever again.'

That was when Alex felt the world turn and stand neatly on its head. 'Wh-what?'

His hand slid under the dark jacket of her neat business suit. With intimidating expertise, he flicked the buttons of her blouse aside. Alex held her breath.

'And you will never call yourself a "soppy spinster" in my hearing.'

His fingers were devastatingly cool on warm flesh. She felt her cotton bra loosen. Her breast seemed to rise of its own accord to meet the questing hand. Alex heard herself moan, a feral sound she would not have believed she was capable of.

Suddenly, Joe dropped his head. She thought she felt his lips in her hair. She was not sure because she was trembling, suspended on the brink of a sensation she sensed would overwhelm her.

She clung to him. She could hear her own breathing, like a wild animal in the silent room. Her fingers flexed like claws against the cloth of his sleeve. Her head fell back. She felt his lips on her throat, her exposed collarbone, her breast. She writhed, needing more, needing…needing…

I want him.

His mouth closed over her nipple.

Needing *that*. She gasped. It was like a scream.

He made a satisfied sound deep in his throat. Alex registered it with a queerly distant triumph. Her arms closed round him fiercely. They were too driven to stand upright a moment longer, but Joe lowered her to the floor with a care she was only dimly aware of. All she knew was that his mouth was driving her upwards, onwards, farther than she had ever been, towards…towards…

She convulsed, shuddering, and went on shuddering, with little eddies of diminishing sensation, while he held her. It felt, thought Alex, like real tenderness. With a little sigh of complete surrender, she let her head fall against his shoulder. Her mind was quite empty. Her body was utterly relaxed.

She thought muzzily, *I feel wonderful.*

She found she had said it aloud.

Joe's arms tightened. She realised that he was holding her cradled against his body. One hand combed lazily through her hair, lifting it to the light and letting it fall with a mesmeric rhythm. Alex thought she had never felt so happy in her life.

She stopped her dreamy drifting right there. Hell, she could have said *that* aloud too. She went hot at the mere thought.

He felt the change in her muscles.

'Cramp?' he said, his voice warm with laughter.

'Dusty,' corrected Alex.

She struggled to sit up, pulling her clothes together as best she could. She kept her back to him. She did not think she could meet his eyes. She did not know what she most dreaded to see there: laughter or intimacy. She had no idea how to deal with either. Especially as, God help her, they were both justified. Now.

I wish I were more experienced at this sort of thing, thought Alex, trying not to wince.

She scrambled to her feet, not very gracefully. Her navy skirt had attracted a good deal of powdery dust, some fluff and a singularly persistent paperclip. She made a business of brushing it down, glad of the excuse to keep her hands busy and her eyes off Joe Gomez.

Her body, indulged though it had been, was now reminding her that she still wanted him and they still had a long, long way to go on the path of sensual discovery. If he wanted her too, of course. Alex refused even to think about that.

She said brightly, 'All right. You proved your point. I'm not a robot. Well done.'

There was a little silence. Alex tucked her shirt back into the waistband of her skirt and patted her jacket into place. She kept her back to him.

Joe said very quietly, 'Excuse me?'

'You win. According to my grandmother, that's what you always want.'

He pulled her round to face him.

Alex met his eyes with a faint smile. It was an effort, but she managed it.

The hand on her arm tightened until she could have cried out. She did not make a sound.

He said, 'How well you think you know me.'

Gone were the charmer, the teasing pirate and the red-hot lover alike. Instead, just for the moment, he sounded so bleakly weary that Alex almost wished it unsaid. Almost.

And then he released her, turning away to his desk.

'Well, if I've proved you're not a soppy spinster, I guess I haven't lived in vain.'

The laughing pirate was back with a vengeance. Alex flushed vividly. She decided that she hated him. 'Am I supposed to say "thank you"?' she snapped, tidying her own desk with angry jabs. She almost threw the neat trays of paper into the cupboard behind her.

'Not necessarily,' Joe assured her kindly.

'Pah!' She slammed the door on the day's correspondence with unnecessary vigour.

Joe strolled over and sat on the corner of the desk. If anyone came in, she thought, they would see two colleagues chatting casually as they closed up for the day. Only Alex, her blood still tumultuous, saw that his eyes were not casual, and knew that her own were not either.

What is happening to me? She straightened.

'But I do think you owe me an explanation,' Joe said thoughtfully.

Alex braced herself and told the truth. 'Lust. Pure and simple. Sorry.'

He blinked. Then, unholy laughter gleamed in his eyes. 'I'm flattered,' he said with grave courtesy. 'But that wasn't what I meant.'

Oh no! Another stupid blunder! What an idiot he must think I am.

Alex fought embarrassment down with a mighty effort. She watched him warily. 'What then?'

'Why you . . .' he hesitated, choosing his words, 'seem to put yourself down all the time.'

Alex blenched. Joe saw it, adding, 'Not tonight,' as if he

was agreeing with something she had said. 'We're too wired to make sense of anything. Both of us. Cold light of day is what we need. But we will talk. And soon.'

She swallowed. 'OK,' she said, meaning *not on your life*.

Joe smiled down at her as if he could read her mind.

'That's a promise,' he said gently. 'I know you keep yours. This is where you learn that I keep mine.'

And then he got up and strolled out, quite as if he had never had his hands on her naked skin or his tongue in her mouth. As if he had never challenged her or made her look away from him in an agony of need. As if he had never turned her world upside-down.

Alex looked after him, shivering. She felt lost and bewildered. And very, very lonely.

The loneliness persisted when she got home. Julie was out, rehearsing. She had just landed the lead in *Peter Pan*, and the press night was imminent. As a result, Alex rarely saw her.

She tried to call Rupert, but he was still in a huff. When she could not offer any better explanation of her call than that she was missing him, he unbent a little. But not enough to offer to come over.

'You must realise, I can't just drop everything on one of your whims, Alex,' he announced. 'I have other things in my life. Responsibilities. Besides, you agreed that we would not see each other so much before Christmas,' he reminded her.

Alex had the distinct impression that he was secretly pleased by her call. He interpreted it to mean that she was at last seeing the error of her ways.

She felt like the little girl she had been when they first met. Her parents had hated each other so much by that time that her mother was hitting out physically, while her father would storm off in his big, off-road vehicle and drive round the country lanes for hours, leaving her mother raging. Rupert, a magnificent ten-year-old living in the nearest house, had let

Alex trail after him. She got dirty and scratched and, after a couple of times when he had made her climb big trees, really scared. But at least she had a companion, however indifferent.

Alex said in a low voice, as much to herself as to him, 'I really, really don't want to be alone tonight.'

'Then maybe we should reinstate our former arrangement,' said Rupert pompously. 'Think about it. I'll call you at the weekend.'

He hung up.

Alex spent an unsettled evening slumped in front of the television. Eventually, she couldn't think of another reason not to go to bed, though she dreaded the dreams even more than the loneliness.

The dreams were exactly what she expected. The flambeaux. The empty room. The mirror. And the man.

This time he was wearing a mask, a white Venetian carnival mask. It hid all of his face except his eyes.

Alex could not look away from those eyes. They were unfathomably dark, and seemed to be sending her a message. She stared and stared, but she could not make it out.

Was it a challenge? A threat? Or something quite different?

She tried to ask, 'What do you want?' but no sound came out.

He held out his hand, and she saw he was wearing one of those billowing carnival cloaks and long black gloves that ended in points at the elbow. Only his eyes were uncovered, and they burned. They burned.

She put her hand into his gloved one. She could feel the warmth of his bone and muscle under the velvet. He never took his eyes off her as he walked through the mirror towards her, and they ran like ghosts down the sweep of staircase into the street. She tried to turn to him, but he would not let her.

But she felt those hands, too hard and strong for a ghost, on her shoulders as he turned her away from him. She felt the warmth of him at her back, although the street and the night were cold.

There was a billow of silk cloak as he bent forward, a waft of warmth along her cheek, the sudden harshness of his hair against the nape of her neck, and then a mouth at her throat.

She knew who it was. She said his name, slowly, wonderingly, trying to turn towards him, but then he flew away from her. Down the elegant street, faster than a bullet. She watched him go, not believing it. She heard his laugh echoing in the cold night air.

When Alex woke up, there were tearstains on her face. And she still knew who he was.

'Oh boy, am I in trouble,' she said aloud.

chapter six

Joe went running at his usual time. It was where he and Tom usually met these days.

'How's it going?' asked Tom, puffing along beside him.

'I've got an outline for the Venice programme. I'll be sending it round by the end of the week. Just ideas for the follow-ups as yet.'

'That's fine,' said Tom. Now that he had a task to focus on, he was the old Tom, thought Joe, relaxed and confident. 'That's all we need. We're selling it on the back of Venice. The Japanese loved the idea.'

'Alex said they would.'

'That's why they signed in the end.' Tom was moved to enthusiasm. 'She's a marvel, your Alex, isn't she?'

'She is,' agreed Joe levelly. 'Though she's not mine.'

He did not like saying it. It surprised him how much he did not like saying it. Joe had never been possessive. For one thing, he was a modern man; women weren't possessions. For another – well, if you laid claim to something, you also had to take care of it. Joe liked to steer clear of commitments like that. Independent women who took care of themselves without any help from a man had always suited him very well.

Except that Alex, so impeccably independent in every way, somehow seemed to bring out his protective instincts. He actually ... wanted to take care of her.

Take last night, for instance. She had looked so astonished when he kissed her. He had done it on impulse. He was so angry, and he'd wanted to shake her up.

But when she'd looked at him like that – when she'd shouted 'Get off!' and looked like a thwarted teenager – all he had wanted to do then was to take her in his arms. More than that, he had wanted to make love to her until she woke up to the fact that she was an adult woman, and he wanted that so badly he hurt.

And, God help him, he bloody nearly had.

Except that she was not 'his' Alex. She was Rupert Sweet-croft's Alex, as she had reminded him last night. Reminding him at the same time, with every word she said, that Sweet-croft was a toe-rag who did not deserve her.

I could deserve her, thought Joe. If I put my mind to it. I could make her happy. If I could only find a way through.

Alex could not make up her mind whether to go to work early or not. She had to face Joe Gomez. She knew that. More importantly, he knew it. What he didn't know, of course, was that she had been dreaming about him. Facing him with last night's dream dancing about at the edge of her memory was not a prospect she relished.

Alex tried hard to be sensible about it. That's what she did best, after all, she thought bitterly. She was good at 'sensible'.

It was reasonable enough that she should dream about Joe. She saw him every day. There were times when she saw him *all* day, for Heaven's sake. She could not avoid thinking about him. Especially as, when she did get away from work at last, her whole family were continually talking about him.

'Hell, with exposure like that, the man must have a season ticket to my dreams,' she said aloud.

And then she remembered: she had been dreaming about him *before* she worked with him every day. She had been dreaming about him before he had even kissed her!

She found she could not face going into work early. In fact, she found she could not face going to work at all. Probably for the first time in her life, she was running scared.

Alex was still considering the prospect bleakly over her morning coffee cup when Julie trailed into the kitchen. She stopped.

'Hello,' she said astonished. 'What's wrong?'

'Nothing,' said Alex, pursing her lips over her disquieting secrets.

Julie shrugged and draped herself over the breakfast bar, eyes closed, while she waited for the kettle to boil.

She had never run away from anything, thought Alex. *Never.* Not even when her mother had said she would kill herself if Alex visited her father in his new home. She had always known it was best to turn and walk *towards* the things she was scared of.

So what was happening to her now? She was not afraid of Joe Gomez, surely?

Oh, but she was! She was afraid of what he made her dream! And not just dream. Alex tried not to. But she could not help remembering the way she had responded to him last night.

Responded, hell! She had offered herself. What else could you call it? She had arched up to that clever mouth, all voluptuous sensation, not a thought in her head except the stroke of flesh on flesh. And Julie was right. He *did* have the mouth of a red-hot lover. Maybe she should come right out and admit it, thought Alex with bitter self-contempt.

Just thinking about it was enough to make her snort aloud.

Julie jumped, opening her eyes reproachfully.

'Sorry,' Alex said automatically.

The kettle switched itself off. Julie made her own coffee, looked at Alex's preoccupied expression and silently made another cup for her friend. She pushed it across the bar.

'What's wrong?'

Alex gave herself a shake. Compared with what she had heard about some of Julie's adventures, last night was pretty insignificant. OK, she had let down her guard and ended up writhing on the office floor with a man she could not stop dreaming about. But it was not the end of the world. No one but Joe needed to know about her loss of control last night.

And *nobody* needed to know about the dreams.

There, she thought; that's better. Getting it into perspective already.

But she still did not gather up her things and sweep off to work as she usually did, a fact Julie observed with interest. 'What is it, Alex? If you've got a problem, it usually helps to talk, you know.'

Alex was not quick enough to stop herself shuddering at the thought. *No one need know about the dreams.* Julie's eyebrows flew up.

Alex said hurriedly, 'It's work. That's all. Work.'

'By which I presume you mean the gorgeous Joe Gomez.'

There was no point in denying it. 'Er… yes.'

Julie shook her head. 'How any woman can work day in day out with a man who looks like a devil designed by the Medicis, and still claim to be in love with Rupert Sweetcroft, I will never understand.'

'Maybe I don't like devils,' Alex said with spirit.

She encountered a disbelieving look. 'With anyone else I would say she was deceiving herself, but in your case, you could just be right,' Julie admitted. She added in a practical tone, 'What's he done, then?'

'Joe?' By dint of sounding vague and concentrating on the swirl of her coffee, Alex managed not to blush. Just. 'Oh nothing much. Just rushing around taking on too much. Forgetting to tell me he's done it and then getting…er…difficult when I try to take charge of the diary.'

Julie was amused. 'Shoot him,' she advised.

'Don't think I haven't thought about it.'

'Or let him sort out his own brilliant ideas. I thought you were supposed to be a partner – not a dogsbody.'

Alex smiled. She was beginning to feel better. 'It's the same thing, if you work with Joe Gomez.'

'Not a democratic boss, then?'

'Er…no, you could say that.'

'So, you're fiddling about here rehearsing your resignation speech?'

Alex was startled. 'What? Why do you say that?'

'Because I've been watching your lips move,' Julie said dryly.

'Oh,' said Alex. 'Well, not resignation exactly. But trying to think how to play something…er…difficult.'

'Loudly,' said Julie. 'Or Joe won't notice.'

Alex chuckled in spite of herself. Yes, really *much* better. Almost normal, in fact.

'So your advice would be?'

'I don't give advice,' said Julie hastily. 'Not about other people's relationships. With my track record, I'd be a fool to try.'

Suddenly, all desire to laugh left Alex. 'I don't have a *relationship* with Joe!' She sounded shocked, and more than a little anxious.

Julie shrugged. 'There you are, then. I'm definitely not the person to ask. I've even got that wrong,' she added, turning to look out of the window. 'And I think this is where I disappear. Because your non-relationship has just got out of a car, and I wouldn't want to get anything else wrong.'

Alex sprang to her feet. 'What? Oh, I don't believe it. Julie…'

Julie gave her a wide smile and seized her coffee. 'You're on your own, kid. Good luck.'

'AAAAGGGHHH…!' shouted Alex. It was drowned by the ring of the doorbell.

Well, at least she was dressed for work, thought Alex, trying to calm herself. At least he wasn't going to find her falling apart in a dressing gown. She straightened her spine and went to open the door.

Joe did not say anything for a moment, just looked at her searchingly.

He gave a quick puff of relief, as if he had got to the top of a mountain, then came in. After that initial scanning of her expression, he did not hesitate, Alex noted. He certainly did not wait for an invitation.

'OK. What is it? Hot temper, or cold feet?'

As always, he managed to disconcert her. 'Wh-what?'

'After last night,' he explained kindly. 'Are you angry with me, or scared of yourself?

'Neither,' said Alex, beginning to bristle. She closed the door carefully behind him. 'Come in, why don't you,' she said with heavy sarcasm.

'Thank you.'

He brushed past her. It was hardly a touch, more a movement of air that set up microscopic eddies that touched them both. But it stilled Alex.

For a moment, she felt all the things she had felt last night – the heat, the need, the suffocating embarrassment. And then the loneliness.

He looked back at her. The heavy eyebrows made him look as if he was frowning.

'What is it?'

She gave a little shiver. 'Nothing. Let's go into the sitting room, and you can tell me why you're here.'

Joe gave a short laugh. 'That's easy. I wanted to be sure I still had a partner.'

Her head reared up, startled. Alex was shocked. Of all the things that had occurred to her over the last twelve hours, the possibility of dissolving the partnership had never figured.

Joe read her expression. 'That's a relief.'

Alex pulled herself together. 'Of course it was terribly unprofessional,' she said primly. 'I can only come back on the strict understanding that it never happens again.'

It almost sounded as if she had been rehearsing the little speech, instead of plucking it from the air at that very moment.

He looked so gorgeous this morning. He must have been

running. He was in tracksuit trousers and a short-sleeved tee-shirt that revealed muscles she tried not to think about. The dark hair was crisp with dew – or perhaps he was not long out of the shower?

The thought of Joe Gomez in the shower flickered across the inner screen of her imagination. Alex swallowed hard.

He grinned at her as if he could read her mind.

'I won't try to take you on the office floor again,' he said outrageously. 'I'm willing to add a clause to the partnership contract, if you like.'

'Don't be ridiculous,' snapped Alex, trying not to let the image of their bodies entwining follow the unwanted shower scene.

What was happening to her? Her imagination never used to be this unruly. Nor did her temperature control. She pressed a hand to her cheek to see if it was as hot as it felt from the inside. It was. Damn him!

Joe said easily, 'Look on the office-floor scenario as a blip. I've got to go to Venice, anyway. I'll go now. Give you some breathing space. How's that?'

Alex had to admit that it made things easier. Well, it did until a roughly wrapped parcel appeared on her desk.

Alex opened it, surprised.

It was a china mug. On one side there was what looked like a print of a photograph. It was of an elephant at some African waterhole. On the other side of the mug, in neat lettering, was the motto, *Elephants stop work sometimes!* She cradled it, smiling. She was almost sure that Joe had commissioned it specially. She had never seen a mug like that for sale any-where.

There was a card among the wrappings. She picked it up curiously, recognising Joe's bold Gothic script.

'One from the wish list,' it said. And on the other side: 'Forget the office floor.'

Alex dropped it as if it had burned her.

'Forget! Huh!' she muttered. But she could at least smile about it now. *Clever Joe*, she thought, not entirely pleased.

Of course, he'd probably had lots of practice at mending fences with women. She did not know as much about that as she ought to, thought Alex. But, maybe she ought to? Purely for professional reasons, of course. Just so she didn't make any unfortunate mistakes between clients and ex-girlfriends.

In pursuit of this professional objective, she took some photocopies up to the room where they did the technical drawing. It had two great tables, a number of geometric instruments, huge piles of paper of various sizes and fineness, a dartboard – and the betting book.

Alex knew that betting book quite well by now. She put the photocopies down, and flicked idly through the pages.

'Do the girlfriends get a page to themselves?' she asked casually.

Charlie and a lanky Indian genius put down their darts and came over. Charlie took the book away from her.

'Only person who changes girlfriends regularly is Joe,' said the genius. 'No bets are on until he starts to spoil them.'

'Haven't had a runner for months,' added Charlie, returning the book to its shelf and ramming it in hard.

'*Spoil* them? What do you mean?'

'That's what Joe calls it,' explained the genius. He seemed not to notice that Charlie was glaring at him. 'He finds something they like especially – and gets it for them.'

'Like what?'

'Could be anything. Tea at the Ritz. Night at the opera. One girl wanted to sleep over with the dinosaurs at the Natural History Museum!' He laughed heartily.

'Joe is good to lots of people,' said Charlie, dismissively.

'He took her to sleep in the Natural History Museum…?' echoed Alex, ignoring the interruption.

'Yeah. Joe takes a lot of trouble with things like that.'

'Doesn't he, just,' said Alex grimly.

She marched downstairs and thrust the elephant mug into her bottom drawer. She was hot with anger.

When Joe came back, she promised herself… When Joe came back, she would tell him…

But he didn't come back. Instead, he summoned her to Venice.

'What am I doing here?' she muttered, as he marched her up the steps of a mediaeval palace. It was some office of the Town Hall, as far as Alex could see.

'Giving Tom and me credibility.'

'What?'

'The rivals are in town. They're telling the authorities that we're a couple of con men.' Joe looked down at her, his eyes wicked. 'You're here to prove that the company has substance. No one could think you were a con man. Not in a suit like that.'

Alex glared. She handed over copies of the company registration papers to the worried bureaucrats with considerable sympathy.

'I'd think he was a con man, too,' she told them. 'But appearances are deceptive. He actually does deliver.'

'Better believe it,' muttered Joe in her ear.

She ignored him.

He saw that he had to make amends.

'Let me show you round while you're here,' he coaxed. 'I'm good on Venice.'

'You're…' Alex curbed the instinct to tell him exactly what she thought of his mischievous teasing. They had to work together, she reminded herself. 'All right. My flight isn't until seven. Show me the thinking-architect's Venice.'

'I'll give you the full preview,' he promised.

He did more than that. He showed her a new world. Alex had been to Venice before, but she had never seen it as Joe showed it to her.

'Look at the art. Look at the buildings,' he said. 'They were looters. And what they didn't loot, they plagiarised. They were complete scavengers. And they made a magic place.'

'*Venice spent what Venice earned,*' quoted Alex.

Joe was interested. 'I don't know that. What is it?'

'A poem we learned at school, Browning, I think. *What of soul was left I wonder, when the kissing had to stop?*'

'That's good. We might use it. You're an inspiration, my love.'

'Don't call me that.'

But he was not listening. 'We'll take a water-taxi into the lagoon. You see the city best from there. You've got time.'

It was a revelation.

The water heaved and murmured all the time, but it did not feel like either a flowing river or the tidal sweep of the sea. Alex said so.

'That's because it's both. And neither. This is a delta. The lagoon is made up of hundreds of dozens of channels between sand bars. Sailors who don't know it regularly run aground.' He told their boatman to stop, and they turned to look back at the city. He began to name the towers and the foursquare colonnaded palaces.

The sun was beginning to set. It edged the autumn clouds with gold. A sea mist, as insubstantial as vapour, was swirling. Through it the city seemed to come and go in blocks of solid colour – brick and parchment and honey and black. Seagulls wheeled over their heads, crying.

'It feels as if we could fall off the edge of the world,' said Alex slowly.

Joe turned to look at her. 'Scared?'

The boat rocked, unpredictable as the fog. She wanted to reach for his hand to steady her, but repressed the urge.

'Anyone in their right mind should approach a new experience with caution,' she announced.

His face went pirate-wicked. 'Is that so? Well in that case, how about going for the big one?'

'What?'

'Stay the night with me,' he said coolly.

Alex could not believe her ears, though she could feel that they were scarlet.

'I don't believe you,' she choked when she could speak. 'You promised you wouldn't…'

'I promised that we wouldn't make out on the office floor,' he reminded her. 'I can offer you something better than the floor tonight. And as you're all braced up for a new experience…'

She said furiously, 'Don't be stupid. People don't fall into bed on a whim.'

'Yes they do. That's exactly why they fall into bed.'

'I don't see why,' she said scornfully. It was meant to be a put-down, but Joe considered it almost as if she had asked his academic opinion on it.

'Well, sex can tell you a lot. You open up to someone – and see where it leads. Abandon yourself, and you might find the secret of the universe.'

It almost sounded as if he was serious. For a moment, Alex felt an answering leap of the pulse. Then she thought of Rupert.

She said loudly, 'I don't trust mirages.'

Joe sighed. 'You don't trust anything.'

'And how right I was,' said Alex furiously. 'How on earth are we going to work together now?'

'You mean because I want you to abandon yourself?'

'I mean because you just propositioned me,' she yelled. 'And you bought me an elephant mug, too.'

He was silent for a moment. Then he said with a glimmer of a smile, 'I won't apologise for the elephant. But there's a client in Mexico. I can go and see him, if you want a breathing space. Would it help?'

The steam went out of her. 'Yes,' she said. And then, painfully, 'I know it sounds stupid. But I'm a one-man woman, Joe.'

His expression was enigmatic. 'I'll bear it in mind.'

But he did not tease any more. And he went to Mexico.

Alex got her equilibrium back slowly. Then Rupert blew it apart.

At dinner with his friends, he said casually, 'I'm in New York all next week. Big negotiation. Probably won't be back until the weekend after next.'

Alex looked up, alarmed. 'That weekend? But of course you'll be back in time to take me to the dance my father is giving for Laine?' Her voice scraped. She was dreading her half-sister's party and all the attendant tensions and Rupert knew it. 'You promised!'

The other guests looked uncomfortable.

Oh God, I'm being pathetic, thought Alex. Rupert will hate that. I may just have torpedoed my own boat.

And certainly he was frowning. 'I told you that I couldn't put my career on hold for purely social reasons,' he said, irritated. 'Grow up, Alex. It's not the end of the world if I can't get back in time. It isn't as if you won't know anyone there.'

Her hostess, a woman Alex had known and detested at school, brayed with sycophantic laughter. Her husband was trying to negotiate a contract with Rupert's bank.

'I'll do my best,' said Rupert. 'But I can't promise anything.'

This meant that he would miss the dance deliberately, thought Alex. She knew him very well. She knew he had a point to make, but she said nothing. What was the point?

But on the doorstep when he took her back to the house, she was not responsive when he took her into his usual rough embrace.

'Come along, Alex,' said Rupert, grinding her against him

until she thought her ribs would crack. 'Don't sulk.'

Involuntarily, she thought of other arms. Of a mouth that did not accuse, but danced along her throat, her breast, as if every breath was a pleasure. Of the slowly mounting throb of blood and heat. Of a man who said, 'Abandon yourself, and you might discover the secret of the universe.'

It was not Rupert's fault that he was not a red-hot lover, Alex reminded herself fairly. But couldn't he have been a little kinder?

She pushed herself away and held him braced at arm's length. 'I'm sorry. I'm very tired,' she said formally. 'Good night, Rupert.'

She whisked inside before he could argue. She closed the door on him with relief. His expression in the porch light had not been pleasant.

He did not call for some days. Alex was slightly relieved, though she knew she would have to talk to him eventually. If he wasn't going to take her to the dance at her father's house, she had to know whether his invitation to stay with his parents was still open. Nevertheless, she decided to put it off until the following Monday. And by Monday, Joe was due back from Mexico.

He strolled in when she was on the phone to her dinner-party hostess.

She flapped a hand in acknowledgement. He wandered over to the bare pine table that served as his desk and flung himself back in his chair. He folded his hands and watched her, making absolutely no attempt at all to pretend that he was not listening to her telephone conversation.

Alex tried to concentrate. 'Look,' she said in a repressive voice, 'I'm a bit busy at the moment, Kate, and...'

But her former hostess did not notice the hint.

'Darling, you looked so miserable. You hardly opened your mouth. Everything is all right between you and Rupert, isn't it?'

Alex reminded herself that loyalty required she did not say anything to anyone about Rupert that she had not cleared with him in advance.

'Everything's fine with Rupert,' she said firmly.

Joe leaned his chin on his hands and raised one wicked eyebrow. Alex glared at him.

Kate remonstrated further.

'No, honestly,' said Alex in desperation. 'I was just tired. Really. I had a wonderful time. Lovely food, lovely company. Look, Kate, I've got to get some work done. I'll call you.'

She flung the phone back on its hook and sat back. Her wings of dark curls blew visibly in her gusty sigh of relief. There was no comment from the other side of the room. Alex looked across at Joe Gomez. He was laughing openly.

Her irritation deepened. 'Satisfied?' she snarled.

He banished the smile and managed to look soulful.

'I'll only be satisfied when you find a man worthy of you. A one-man woman is wasted on Sweetcroft.'

Alex was not deceived by the soulful look. And she was outraged by the comment, especially after his mischievous suggestion in Venice.

'Like you, I suppose?' she asked sweetly.

Joe pursed his mouth, pretending to consider it. 'You could do worse.'

'No, I couldn't,' Alex said with conviction.

Joe shook his head. This time it was his wounded look. 'Sometimes you can be very cruel, Alex.'

In spite of herself, she grinned. 'Oh no, I can't. I can't even manage rude. If I could bring myself to be rude, I'd have told Rupert that I didn't want to go to Kate's damn party in the first place.'

He surveyed her without much sympathy. 'Then you've only yourself to blame. You know, you'd find life so much easier if you'd only tell the truth.'

Alex gave a helpless shrug. 'Her husband wanted to meet

Rupert,' she said. 'My father would have been upset if I'd chickened out.'

Joe made a face as he always did when Alex mentioned her family. He tolerated her grandmother because she was an achiever like himself. But he made no secret of the fact that he deplored Alex's titled relations and the social circle that went with them. On the one occasion she had introduced him to her father, Joe had been polite to seven degrees of frost.

Now he said restlessly, 'You really ought to try and say "no" sometime.'

Rather to her own surprise, she said deliberately, 'I have no problem with saying "no" when it's important.'

Their eyes met. There was no doubt they were both recalling her rejection of his offer in Venice.

Joe gave a little nod, acknowledging a hit. 'I asked for that,' he said philosophically. 'OK. Tell me why it's so important that Rupert Sweetcroft gets every damned thing he wants.'

She said slowly, 'I've loved Rupert forever. Since I was six, really. He was ten then. Oh, he was magnificent. He won all the prizes at the local point-to-point on a peach of a pony.' She thought about it. 'In fact, in those days I probably loved the pony as much as I loved him. Although he did let me play with his friends.'

Joe's lip curled. 'That was good of him.'

Alex gave a reminiscent smile. 'Well, it was. He could have been horribly teased, with me trailing after him all the time.'

Joe moved restlessly. 'Sounds irresistible.'

'If you had the parents I had, it was,' Alex said dryly. 'In those days, I spent my life creeping about a damned great manor house, with my parents in a permanent state of war. In fact, the only time they noticed me was when I gave them a reason to quarrel.'

At this inopportune moment, Alex's telephone rang. She picked it up.

'Hello?'

'I have Mr Sweetcroft for you,' said Rupert's cut-glass-accented secretary, her pure tones trilling across the room.

Joe sat upright and became even more inscrutable.

'Hello, Rupert,' said Alex, flustered when he came on the line. 'Thanks for calling back.'

'I didn't,' said Rupert disagreeably. 'Fool of a secretary thought you were a business contact. What is it, Alex? Keep it short, I'm on my way to a meeting.'

Joe's face became a mask. There was no doubt that he had heard that, too.

Alex hesitated.

'Next weekend. The dance…' she began.

Rupert made a noise, like a steam kettle that had reached explosion point. 'Oh, not that again. I *told* you!'

Alex felt as if someone had sneaked up behind her and stripped off all her clothes while she wasn't looking. She actually crossed her arms over her breasts.

'No. Not that. I was calling about staying with your parents…'

But Rupert was not listening. 'For Christ's sake, Alex! What do I have to *do*? This is my career we're talking about here. I can't give less than one hundred per cent, just because it clashes with some family party.'

It was unfair, but at the moment, Alex was beyond thinking about fairness or even her own dignity. The cold, angry voice was doing its work.

'Please…' she said in a small voice, 'I…need you.'

Even as she said it, she did not know why she was bothering. It was clear that Rupert was not going to change his mind. There was no point in arguing. He already knew all the reasons, and they did not move him an iota. Alex felt the familiar chill of helplessness take hold. She began to shake.

'Rupert…' It was not much more than a whisper.

He ignored it. He had worked himself up into a fine state of indignation by now. His voice continued, thin and hectoring, on the other end of the telephone.

Alex hardly heard him, and certainly did not take in what he said.

She was going to have to go into the lions' den on her own! She was going to have to go alone!

She felt sick.

A hand reached across her neat desk and quietly took the telephone out of her hand.

'Enough, already,' said Joe evenly.

He returned the handset to its place. For once, he was not laughing. The wolf was very apparent. From the set jaw to narrowed and glittering eyes, he looked coldly, implacably angry.

Alex flushed and pulled herself together. 'Sorry. Sometimes I make a fuss about silly things,' she muttered.

It was what Rupert said all the time. She was astonished when Joe laughed aloud.

He said, 'No, you don't. You don't make a fuss about nearly enough. What has got you on the raw, my love?'

She winced, but she gave him a watery smile as well. Joe could always make things seems less terrible.

'What would it take to stop you listening to my telephone calls?' she asked.

'Two stout walls and a sound-proof door,' Joe said promptly. 'Terrible waste of money. Come on, give.'

She did. She knew him. It was easier.

'All right. It's no big deal. You'll think it's ridiculous, I expect. It's just that my half-sister is having a sort of coming-out party, and I have to go. I wanted Rupert to be there. I need... I need support.' When you put it like that, it sounded feeble, she thought in disgust. Almost as feeble as Rupert had found it. She braced herself for Joe's mockery.

She met his eyes bravely. They were intent. But there was no mockery in them.

'Why?'

Her mouth went dry at the thought of explaining. 'It's complicated. And not very important…'

Joe strolled over to her and took the pen out of her hands. He placed both of her hands in his own and leaned over her.

'You know, Alex, you're a terrible liar,' he said conversationally.

She refused to be intimidated. It was a relief to be angry with someone, she found. She stood up and met him levelly, eye to eye.

'How dare you…'

Still in that same conversational tone, he said, 'Did you know you were crying?'

She was shaken. 'I… what nonsense!'

He put out a hand and drew it very gently down her cheek to the corner of her mouth. Alex stood stock still, inexplicably shocked.

'Tear stain,' he explained.

'Oh.' Caught out, Alex looked away.

Joe took her hands and gave them a gentle shake. 'Come on, Alex. You're not the sort of girl who cries for nothing. Are you going to tell me? Or do I have to kiss it out of you?'

chapter seven

'*What?*'

Alex stared at Joe, suddenly rocketed into the present. She was shaken to the core, and had no time to hide it. Joe's eyes glinted.

'And I can,' he reminded her softly.

Alex's shock gave way to indignation. He had gone to Mexico, supposedly to give her time to get over her embarrassment in Venice. Now he just lobbed it into the conversation when she least expected it – and was least prepared to respond composedly. As if it was now going to be part of their shared experience, which they would happily refer to whenever they…he…felt like it.

She said with fury, 'Don't you dare talk to me about that episode. Don't you *dare!*'

His eyebrows rose. 'Interesting.'

Alex took a hurried step forward, her fists clenching at her sides.

'Don't you dare call me "interesting". I'm not one of your blasted projects.'

The dark, dark eyes lit with private laughter. 'Oh, I wouldn't say that.'

'I would.' Alex took hold of herself. It never paid to lose your temper with Joe Gomez. It only gave him another advantage, and he used his advantages ruthlessly. She was not going to give him that chance.

There was a pause while he contemplated her. When he spoke, he sounded faintly annoyed.

'You think you know me so well, don't you, Alex?'

'I do know you well. I listen to your employees, I lie to

your clients and I live in your shadow,' she reminded him.

For a moment, he looked disconcerted. Then, reluctantly, he laughed. 'All right. I'll give you that.'

She nodded.

'But you still don't know me as well as you think you do,' he went on, 'which seems to work both ways.'

Alex frowned, not understanding.

Joe continued, 'So, are you going to tell me what that despair is about? Or am I going to have to go back to Plan B?'

He meant it. It was almost unbelievable, but slowly Alex recognised that Joe was saying nothing less than what he meant to say. If she did not tell him everything he wanted to know, he would come prowling round the desk like a wolf on the scent of prey and kiss her until…

She swallowed hard. Oh, he was smiling easily enough. If Fran walked in now, she would think they were having one of their regular arguments, half-practical, half-teasing. But they were not, and Alex knew it. Her incredulity turned into something close to alarm.

'You're joking,' she said hopefully.

The vulpine eyebrows rose. 'Try me.'

Alex knew that tone of voice. He was not joking. She bit her lip, as Joe watched her.

'It would be easier if you just tell me,' he suggested. He sounded amused, but quite, quite determined.

He moved in closer, took her chin in one hand and tilted her face up to meet his wicked eyes.

'Well?'

For no reason at all, Alex felt the floor lurch under her feet. 'I'll tell you,' she said hurriedly. 'Let me go.'

Joe's expression sharpened. The dark eyes grew intent. His lips parted. The floor showed every sign of giving way terminally. Alex took hold of his wrist and wrenched without success. His grip was iron. Her pulses raced in a response that was purely animal, which shook her.

'Let me *go*, Joe,' Alex gasped. 'I give in. Anything you want to know. Honestly. Just let me go, *please*.'

He did – reluctantly, it seemed. Alex decided not to think about that. She smoothed her hair and shook herself a little.

The floor returned to stability. She wasn't going to think about that either. At least, not just at the moment.

She expected he would move away, now that he had won his point; go back to his desk and fire questions at her from across the room. He did not. Instead, he perched on the corner of her desk and folded his arms across his chest.

'So tell. Why don't you want to go to the party?'

Alex looked away. 'I don't know where to start,' she said lamely.

'Try the beginning. This sister, for a start. I never knew you had a sister. Grandmothers, yes, by the bucketful. And a couple of weird parents. Sisters, no.'

In spite of her uncertain emotions, Alex gave a little choke of laughter at this. She knew that Joe had been brought up by his father, an itinerant oilman, but that his father had died in an accident when Joe was thirteen. Since then, one way or another, Joe had shifted for himself. With the exception of Lavender, he regarded Alex's family, when he had bumped into them, with something between fascination and horror.

She sobered quickly enough. Laine's existence was not something she found easy – either to think about or to describe. She laced her fingers together, watching them absorbedly as she tried to martial her thoughts.

'Only one. Half-sister, actually.' She was conscious of Joe's eyes on her. She did not know what he was thinking. She did not look at him.

After a pause he asked, 'Not close?'

She did look up at him then, her eyes wide and defensive. 'No. I don't really know her. We've never lived together.'

But he was not mocking, as she half-feared. He looked

interested, and unusually serious. Alex let out a small explosion of a sigh before continuing.

'My mother made my father wait for a divorce,' she said abruptly. 'And then discovered that he and his girlfriend already had a child, Laine, who was born when he was still married to my mother.'

She had never talked about it before. It had always seemed disloyal. Now that she had said it aloud, it felt like taking off tight shoes.

Joe made a sympathetic noise. 'Nasty?'

'Oh yes,' she said dryly. 'It was nasty, all right. My father is very sentimental. Laine's mother was – very determined. My mother wouldn't face up to facts. She kept hoping he would come back to us. Pointless, of course. If somebody doesn't want you, there's no point in hanging on. All it does is make the whole thing worse.'

'Is that what happened?'

'Too right. Everyone in the family took sides and declared war.'

Joe blinked. 'Explain.'

Alex sighed wearily. 'My grandfather changed his will. He left Hope House to my grandmother. Then it comes to me. Cuts my father out completely. He's never got over it. He loved the place.'

Joe was unimpressed. 'Don't see a problem. He's still got a roof over his head.'

'Yes but he spent all his cash on it. Laine's mother insisted. So he's now living in a Victorian Gothic house, and the "roof over his head" is leaking. Meanwhile all the capital was put in a discretionary Trust. Lavender won't let the trustees give him any money. Says its all for me. Makes me feel great!'

'You're making me glad I never inherited anything,' Joe said dryly.

She shrugged. 'Yes, it's not all joy being a rich girl. Dad manages. But these days the bank keeps asking for more security.'

Joe's eyes narrowed. 'And you're the security?'

Alex picked up her pen and began to play with it. Joe leaned forward and took it out of her hands. She looked up and read determination in the squared jaw.

'That's it, isn't it? Tell me the truth, Alex.'

She gave in, rather to her own surprise. 'I do what I can. It's only fair.'

'*Fair*!' He made it sound like a crime.

'I talk to the Trustees. Sometimes they'll listen to me. When they don't, I visit and talk to the banks.'

'Visit? How does Lavender take that? And your mother?'

Alex looked depressed. 'I try to play no favourites, but...'

'You know, you're giving me lots of reasons for *not* going to this damned dance.'

Alex shrugged. 'No favourites,' she said again.

The door opened and a head poked round it. Joe looked up impatiently.

'Yes?' He was curt to the point of rudeness.

Fran was used to his abruptness when he was working. It did not worry her any more. She looked anxiously at Alex, saw she was all right and came into the room.

'Hawthorns have rung three times,' she said cheerfully. 'They want to talk to Alex about the revisions estimate. I said she'd be free later this morning.'

'Wrong,' Joe said coolly. 'Call them back and say Alex won't be able to talk to them till tomorrow. She's in conference all day.'

That was something Fran was not used to. It was usually Joe who had her fending off callers with the excuse that he was in conference. Alex took her calls like a trooper.

'But...' she began, startled.

'All day,' Joe said firmly.

'That's not necessary,' Alex said, equally startled, even though she was touched by his gesture.

'Oh yes it is. When you have a problem, light of my life, this whole partnership has a problem,' Joe announced. 'If we're going into it in depth, we need the whole day. See to it, Fran.'

Behind his back the girl made a questioning face at Alex. But Alex was looking at Joe.

'The whole *day*?'

'At the very least.' It was not a tone that encouraged argument.

A thought occurred to him. 'We'll need to eat. Book us a table somewhere, will you, Fran? Decent food, discreet table where we can't be overheard.'

Fran cast her eyes to heaven. It was not the first time she had had such instructions, but the lady on the other side of the table had never been Alex. She was as aware as the rest of the office of the conscientiously impersonal relationship between her two bosses.

'And the moon's made of green cheese and the world ends on Friday,' she muttered.

Joe turned his head and looked at her. She switched on her biggest smile.

'Sure thing, boss.' She went.

'Why did you do that?' Alex asked, annoyed. 'Fran is the most frightful gossip. Now they'll all think…'

'What?' He laughed down at her, the dark eyes challenging. It was her eyes that fell first.

'That you, that I… well, that we're not being very professional,' she muttered, discomfited.

'I'm being completely professional,' Joe said blandly. 'I want to keep the mainstay of the business on the rails. If it takes a champagne lunch, then it's champagne poured in a good cause.'

Alex shook her head. 'You're crazy,' she said with resignation.

'Return to the point,' he urged. 'Your father had just

entered stage left.'

Alex sipped her cooling coffee. In spite of herself, she smiled. Joe had a way of making a disaster look like something that had come about entirely for his amusement.

'He's not the demon king,' she protested.

'He sounds like…' He bit it off. 'Never mind. He is pressurising you to go to this dance. Why?'

'I didn't say that.

His tone was dry. 'You didn't have to.'

Alex sighed. 'Well, he's got a point. Laine's part of the family, too.'

Joe's eyes were suddenly alert.

'Money,' he said softly. 'You said that was what it was about. Are you supposed to pay for this damned dance?'

Alex jumped. Why did she never remember how clever he was?

'That's part of it,' she admitted at last.

'And the rest? What does he want you to do? Buy the girl a house, or a husband?'

Alex was annoyed, and let it show. 'Don't be so archaic. I gather she wants to study in Madrid. It's fair enough that the Trust should pay the bill. Heaven knows, we can afford it. My father thinks…'

'Your father,' said Joe with icy precision, 'thinks that if you go down to this dance and pretend to be reconciled, your trustees will sign on the dotted line.'

Alex was drinking coffee. At this masterly assessment she choked. It had taken her father three phone calls, two letters and three-and-a-half hours in an Italian restaurant to get that message across to his reluctant daughter. She spluttered. Joe thumped her helpfully on the back.

'That's about the size of it,' she agreed when she got her breath back.

Joe said something that did not sound very complimentary under his breath, before adding, 'Is he right?'

Alex shrugged. 'Maybe. I haven't drawn anything from the Trust since I bought my own house, so I don't really know what the Trustees are likely to think. The only certain thing is that my father can't pay for her himself. If there's a chance… well, I can't torpedo it just because I'm too petty to let bygones be bygones.'

Joe's eyes narrowed. 'That sounds like a direct quote.'

Alex jumped. Not for the first time she was shocked by how acute he was.

'Maybe,' she said, deliberately vague. It was a phrase that her father had flung at her in the restaurant when, hedging, she had said she would think about it. She had not been able to get it out of her mind ever since.

There was a little silence. Not, felt Alex, an approving silence.

'You know what's wrong with you?' Joe said at last in his most amiable tone.

Alex swallowed. It was a tone she knew.

'No,' she said wearily. 'But I'm sure you have a full diagnosis.'

'Oh, I have. I have.'

He put down his coffee cup and swung round on her, thrusting his face into hers. It so startled Alex that, in pure reflex, she scooted her chair back until it hit the wall. Joe's eyes were giving off little yellow sparks, like a fire just catching light. Suddenly, he looked as if he was in a towering rage. It was rather alarming. Alex stared at him and kept her mouth shut on the grounds of self-preservation.

'What's wrong with you,' he said, one long finger stabbing at her accusingly, 'is a high susceptibility to guilt, coupled with a totally inadequate value of yourself. Why the hell didn't you tell the whole shooting match to go and fight their duels without involving you?'

'But…'

'Don't interrupt,' said Joe furiously. 'Let them get on with it. It's nothing to do with you if your father wants to chisel some money out of your family Trust.'

Alex sighed. 'I wish.'

'Wishing has nothing to do with it. That's the plain truth.'

'You don't understand…'

'I understand perfectly. It's none of your business,' Joe said, smiting his fist down on her desk so hard that the paper-clips on her desk jumped like fleas.

'It is my business if the trustees are my grandmother's friends, and they won't give it to him because they think they are fighting my battle,' Alex said quietly.

That stopped him. He turned on her. Alex sustained his glare steadily. After a moment, the anger died out of his eyes.

'Good old Alex,' he said ruefully. 'Always seeing the other guy's point of view.' He touched her cheek again briefly, as if he could not help himself. 'Can't expect you to change char-acter just because you're being pushed around by your appalling family, can I?'

Alex was startled into silence. Joe did not seem to notice. He was removing himself from her desk, striding across the parquet with that impatient step she knew. It meant that he was getting an idea. She looked at him with some trepidation. Joe's ideas were unpredictable.

'You'd better tell me when this jamboree is.'

He was leaning over his own desk, flipping through the ele-gantly bound diary that had been a Christmas gift from a grateful bank client. Alex stared at the long, lean back and thought she must be hallucinating.

'What did you say?'

'If I'm to come with you, you'd better give me the date,' he said patiently.

She *was* hallucinating. 'But you hate things like that.'

He turned and looked over her shoulder, grinning. 'So do you,' he pointed out with reason.

'But…'

'Alex,' he said patiently, 'you don't want to go. I don't want to go. You feel you have to go. The Sweetcroft pillock just chickened out. You need support. You've got it.'

She stared at him. He gave her his most mischievous grin.

'If this is a family war, I just joined the expeditionary force. I'm coming too, my love.'

He went on saying it through the rest of the morning. Alex moved from straightforward disbelief to acute discomfort. In fact, she was quite surprised how hard she tried to talk him out of it. Joe was amused, although he pretended to be offended.

'*Need*, Alex. You said you *needed* Rupert there,' he reminded her. 'Are you saying I'm no good as a substitute – even when you clearly need some help?'

'Yes. No. You're trying to make me say something I don't mean,' protested Alex.

'I'm trying to find out what Rupert Sweetcroft has that I haven't got,' Joe said, sounding hurt.

She glared at him. 'Nothing at all, as you are perfectly well aware,' she snapped. It was disloyal to Rupert, but what the hell, she thought. It was also the truth.

Joe chuckled. He had not really been in any doubt about it, Alex thought in dudgeon. Anyway, he was not the sort of man to need reassurance of his attractions from every woman he came across. He had just made her admit it for some private amusement of his own. Now that she had, he was looking particularly wolfish – wolfish and triumphant.

He saw her expression and rapidly composed his own to one of modest regret. It was not very successful. Joe Gomez had never been modest in his life. He saw her eyes kindle, and made a decisive move before she could open hostilities.

'We'll talk it through over lunch,' he said hastily.

Fran had booked them into Garrett's. Either she or the restaurant had taken Joe's instructions literally. They were shown by a hushed-voiced waiter to an alcove surrounded by a trellis covered in greenery. He held her chair for her with the solemn respect of a courtier encountering visiting royalty.

'Everyone will think you're planning a takeover, at least,' Alex told Joe, torn between amusement and a faint awkwardness she could not account for.

He smiled. 'Maybe I am.'

She looked at him sharply, but he was already engaged in a low voiced conversation with the waiter. The man retreated, looking, if possible, even more respectful.

'Now, tell me why you'd rather have Rupert Sweetcroft on your arm than me,' Joe said calmly, all the mock outrage banished.

Alex twitched her shoulders. 'That's not fair.'

'Yes it is. There has to be reason. I'm cleverer, better-looking and a lot more fun,' Joe pointed out. 'So it can't be that.'

In spite of herself, she was surprised into a laugh.

'Could it be that he's less of an egotist?' she suggested dryly.

His eyes crinkled up at the corners, as they always did when he was laughing secretly.

'Not a chance.'

Remembering Saturday night's scene on her doorstep, Alex was inclined to agree with him. All desire to laugh left her abruptly. She looked away.

'I dare say you're right,' she said, with an effort at lightness.

The waiter arrived bringing champagne. It was only after the ceremony of uncorking and pouring had been completed that Alex had a clear look at the label. She gasped.

'*Vintage?*'

'You're the best partner I've got,' Joe said coolly. 'It's in my own best interests to spoil you rotten.'

Alex abandoned the idea of protesting at his extravagance. Instead, she took a sip of the cool, fizzing champagne. It was delicious.

'Thank you,' she said gravely.

'My pleasure.'

He smiled at her. It was a real smile that lit his dark eyes with green highlights. It made him look less like an unpredictable genius, and more like a living, breathing man. Alex found herself smiling back.

Joe drew a long breath. 'You should do that more often.'

It was so unexpected that she was not sure he had said what she thought she heard.

'I'm sorry?' she said blankly.

'Skip it.' He tapped the leather-bound menu. 'What do you want to eat? Remember, this is pure indulgence, and consult only your fantasies. This one's on me. I won't bill the business, I promise.'

Alex chuckled and abandoned herself to the delights of a four-star menu. When they had both chosen, Joe leaned forward.

'You still haven't told me why I'm trailing the field to a third-rate merchant banker with an incipient double chin.'

Alex sighed. No one had ever said Joe was not persistent.

'Don't be ridiculous. You never entered the race,' she said crossly. 'You and I agreed that we had to keep the relationship on a professional footing at all times. Besides...'

His eyes glinted. 'Besides...?'

She had been going to say that on his track record, he would never have looked at a plain, unsophisticated girl like her. But it sounded too much like she was fishing for a compliment. After all, the poor man could hardly agree, could he?

So, instead she said, 'We live in different worlds, Joe.'

His eyebrows flew up. 'All through the working day, we live in the same room, for God's sake.'

'Oh well, work,' said Alex dismissively.

'You think dinners with the likes of your friend, Kate, are

closer to reality?'

'Kate is a very old friend…' she began, ice edging her tones.

He interrupted. 'No she isn't. She's a contact on a network. Your father is on it. Sweetcroft, too, I imagine. But you're not. And you don't want to be.'

Alex was utterly silenced. It was horribly close to the truth.

Joe met her eyes. In spite of his lop-sided grin, she had the feeling that he was not really amused.

'You know, for an intelligent woman, my love, you're not very clued up about people.'

She stiffened. 'What do you mean?'

He looked at her for a long, long moment. Looked deep into her eyes, as if she was supposed to read something in them. Alex shifted restlessly. 'What?' she challenged him.

He said at last, 'You don't want to network. You hate the whole business.'

Alex absolutely *knew* it was not what he had been going to say.

She answered at random, uneasily. 'I'm not very good at it. But that doesn't mean I hate it.'

'Yes it does. Tell any lies you like to Rupert Sweetcroft, but don't lie to yourself,' he said bluntly. 'Or to me.'

Alex swallowed.

He shook his head. 'I still don't understand. Why Rupert? He doesn't appreciate you…'

'What's to appreciate?' said Alex wryly. She had been avoiding looking at her tousled waves in the restaurant's mirror wall all during lunch.

He ignored that. 'He hasn't even put a ring on your finger. Doesn't he think he needs to make sure of you?'

She flushed.

'And don't bother to tell me you sleep with him,' said Joe impatiently. 'That might be a lot of things, but it isn't a commitment. On either part.'

Alex studied the pattern on the linen tablecloth absorbedly. 'I know,' she said at last in a low voice.

'Then *why?*' He sounded exasperated.

She spread her hands helplessly. 'Some people just are one-man women. That's me. I've known Rupert all my life. He…knows me. I don't have to pretend with him.'

Joe surveyed her, his expression suddenly unreadable.

'Don't you? I thought love was all about having to pretend,' he drawled. 'And tell lies and hide and give chase? That's what makes it exciting. That's what makes it fun. What sort of love affair is it that doesn't have any pretence?'

Alex was annoyed. 'An honest one,' she flashed.

He looked disbelieving. 'Honest? Come on, Alex, you've got to know better than that. Honesty is the death knell of a love affair. Any love affair.'

She stiffened. 'Honesty has never killed off any of my love affairs,' she said grandly.

She encountered a look full of irony. 'There's an answer to that, but I'm too much of a gentleman to say it.'

She flushed angrily. 'I don't think you're an authority on love, however much you might know about affairs.'

His eyes flickered, but he said nothing.

Goaded, Alex said rashly, 'I don't suppose you've ever been honest with any of your…' Realising the depths into which she was straying, she broke off abruptly.

Her colour rose even higher. Now she would have really made him angry, Alex thought. When he was angry, Joe's tongue was deadly. It was no help to know she had deserved a tongue-lashing. She braced herself.

Joe, however, was looking unforgivably amused. 'My…?' he prompted gently.

Alex made a despairing gesture. 'Oh, this is so embarrassing. Forget it. I shouldn't have said anything.'

'You certainly shouldn't if you weren't prepared to finish it,' he agreed equably. 'Rule one in conducting an argument,

Alex. In fact, just like a love affair, if you think about it. Never start anything you aren't prepared to finish.'

She felt a fool. She said stiffly, 'I'm sorry. I was out of order.'

'You were…' he broke off suddenly, looking irritated. 'You *are* being extremely evasive. I don't believe you are having an affair with Sweetcroft because you played together as children. Or even because he knows all your horrid family secrets. There's got to be more to it than that. Tell me, Alex.' His voice sank. 'Or I'll embarrass you seriously.'

She looked him in the eye. For all the teasing tone, he was surprisingly grim, she found. Of course, he hated not getting his own way. She swallowed hard and told him the truth.

'Rupert is on my side. He always has been. We're together. If things get tough, I tell myself that it's all right. I'm not alone. I belong to Rupert.'

The dark, mobile, laughing face looked as if it had turned to granite.

'But does Rupert belong to you?'

She was surprised. 'Of course.'

Joe was absolutely silent. He sat so still that for a moment, it seemed as if he had stopped breathing. Alex was alarmed.

Some people react to pain like that, she thought. They go into shock and have to be revived. But she had not said anything that could possibly have caused that reaction in Joe. She stared at him, bewildered. Joe slowly expelled a breath.

'That's quite a belief you've got there.'

Alex felt unaccountably flustered. Her eyes fell. 'Well, you asked,' she said defensively.

'So I did.' His tone was equivocal. 'If I weren't a gentleman, I might be pointing out by now that Rupert has very definitely left you to face the music alone, as far as Laine's dance is concerned. That doesn't look like being on your side to me.'

Alex stared at him. He smiled. The smile got nowhere near

his eyes. 'However, as a master of tact and discretion, I will shelve that delicate issue for another time.'

'Th-thank you.'

'Don't mention it. No point in rubbing it in.' His tone was cordial, but it did nothing to warm up the wintry expression in his eyes.

'Instead, let us think about this practically. Tell me what is involved. What do I have to do to stand in for the love of your life?'

For no reason at all, Alex felt herself go scarlet. The smile reached Joe's eyes at last.

'Just on this one occasion, of course,' he said.

chapter eight

As coolly as she could manage, Alex said, 'There's no need to go too far.'

Joe looked amused. 'And how far is "too far"?'

Alex choked. 'If you're serious, I'll be glad of your escort. And that's *all*.'

He shook his head. 'You can be so hidebound, my love.'

Alex remembered something else that irritated her about him. 'Stop calling me your "love".'

'OK,' he said obligingly. ' "Light of my life". How will that do?'

She shut her eyes briefly. 'Try to be serious,' she begged him. 'Just for a moment.'

'Never been more serious in my life.'

She snorted and opened her eyes. 'You...'

He laughed aloud at that. 'All right, all right. Practicalities. When, where and how? I suppose it's black-tie?'

Alex nodded. 'Do you mind?' she said doubtfully. She knew Joe's views on all forms of pretension.

Joe struck a heroic attitude. 'If I can dress up like a penguin to address my brother architects, I can dress up like a penguin for you.'

Alex narrowed her eyes at him, bewildered.

'The Association Dinner,' he reminded her patiently. 'My speech. To be more precise, the speech you wrote. Tonight. You're booked to give me love, support and laughs in all the right places. You can't have forgotten.'

'Oh, good grief, is that tonight?'

'It is.'

'Oh Joe, I'm sorry, I...' she faltered.

'You're not getting out of it,' he said calmly.

Rupert, she thought, would have flung a tantrum at the first sign of her starting to back out. Joe simply gave his slanted smile and waved her objections away.

'I've got so much work…'

'You have,' he agreed cordially. 'Leading the cheering crowds.'

'I haven't got time to get my hair done.'

He flicked a measuring look over her. 'Wash it and leave it loose.'

'But I've…'

'…Got nothing to wear,' he supplied, laughing.

Alex made a face. 'Yes, I was going to say that,' she admitted.

'You just think you haven't,' he said soothingly. 'We'll go and look.'

Alex jumped. 'What do you mean?'

'What I say. We'll have a look. And if you really haven't got anything to wear, we'll buy you something this afternoon.'

She was outraged. 'Are you proposing to inspect my wardrobe?'

But Joe was not listening. He was already signalling for the bill. Alex knew that expression. He was fired with enthusiasm. She had a nasty feeling that he was determined to turn her into a fashion item, and her heart sank. She knew what he was like when he determined to do something.

But when he stood in her tidy bedroom and flicked his way through her clothes, he looked thoughtful rather than determined.

'Well?' she said uneasily.

'For a rich girl, you don't indulge yourself much, do you? Not a single designer label in sight.'

Alex shrugged. 'My father's second wife is the one for designer labels.'

'Ah.'

She looked at him suspiciously. 'What does "Ah" mean?'

He chuckled. 'You're not naturally dowdy. You're smug.'

'*What?*'

'As bad a case of moral superiority as ever I've seen.'

'That's not true.'

Joe leaned in the window bow and folded his arms over his chest. He was looking interested. 'Don't worry about it. It's a good sign.'

Alex could have danced with fury. 'You know, sometimes I think you must be the most obnoxious man I've ever met.'

'No,' he said. 'The second-most obnoxious.' His eyes sent her a laughing challenge. 'You fell in love with the leader of the pack.'

Alex was outraged. 'You've got no reason to say that.'

One eyebrow flicked up. 'Who's holding your hand at your sister's dance?'

Why, thought Alex fuming, *was he always so damned logical?*

'OK,' she flung at him. 'You've got no *right*. How's that?'

His mouth tightened for a moment. 'Oh, if we're talking rights, I resign utterly. No contest. Except that he really should buy you that ring.'

Alex was not sure whether she had won that round or not. She decided to pretend she had, anyway. She inclined her head like a dowager receiving an apology.

'Thank you.'

He gave a sudden laugh. 'Don't thank me yet. I haven't started.'

'Started?'

Their eyes locked, hers wide and suddenly wary, his amused. Alex became aware that, in spite of its neatness and impersonal furnishing, it was her bedroom they were standing in. She drew back, disconcerted.

Joe smiled. He looked very pleased with himself all of a

sudden. 'But I will,' he said, lounging away from the window and going back to the open cupboard.

His fingers flicked a couple of dresses along the rail disparagingly. Then he found something he liked. He pulled it out and threw it on the bed. 'This,' he said emphatically.

Alex had no trouble in interpreting his expression. Well, maybe 'liked' was too strong a word, she thought ruefully. Something he would put up with.

She picked the dress up.

'This?' She was doubtful.

It was a slim tube, embroidered with black, blue and silver spangles. It had a midnight-blue velvet rose on one shoulder and bootlace straps. She had bought it for a 1920s party several years ago, and had never quite managed to bring herself to throw it away. But it was not at all her usual style.

'Isn't it a bit…well…theatrical?'

Joe's eyes glinted. 'Not the way you'll wear it.'

Alex sighed. 'Go on. Tell me what's wrong with the way I'll wear it.'

He chuckled. 'You won't have an aigrette in your hair. Or a diamond-studded bandanna. Or a feather boa.'

'Thank you for the fashion notes,' she said crisply.

'On the other hand…' he let his remark hang in the air, unfinished, tantalising her.

She was suspicious. 'Yes?'

He paused. Then, regretfully, shook his head. 'I don't think I'll tell you.' He was laughing at her. 'Not yet, anyway. Maybe later.'

'I'll look forward to it,' she said, without even trying to sound as if she meant it. She looked at her watch. 'Shouldn't we be getting back? I know Fran is telling everyone I'm in conference this afternoon, but I still have an enormous amount of work to do.'

Joe's eyes crinkled up at the corners as they did when he was deeply entertained. 'Slave driver!'

But he went with her.

In the taxi back to the office he said lazily, 'Have I made you cry off a date?'

'Tonight?' Alex shook her head. 'No. I saw Rupert on Saturday.'

He looked at her curiously. 'Does he ration you?'

'No, of course not. But we're both busy.'

'And of course, you don't date anyone else,' he mused. 'You being a one-man woman and all.'

Alex suspected he was mocking her. 'There's such a thing as loyalty,' she said stiffly.

Joe looked all the way down his elegant nose. 'Indeed there is,' he agreed blandly. 'And sometimes it is misplaced.'

Alex flicked him an irritated look. 'Is this still about my alleged networking for my father?'

'No. It's about your making yourself wretched for your father,' he said tranquilly, stretching his arm lazily along the back of the seat behind her. Alex tipped her head back, sighing.

'Social obligations,' she said, giving up the fight. 'You're right. I hate them.'

Her hair caught on the dark cuff of his sleeve. He looked down at it. An odd smile curled the corner of his mouth. Alex was unaware of it.

'What you need,' he said thoughtfully, 'is just a little bit more resolution.' He lifted her hand from where it was resting on her knee and surveyed it, turning it over look at the palm. 'Why don't you try? It might be easier than you think.'

Alex was startled, and gave a rather uneasy laugh. 'It would run counter to a lifetime of virtue.'

'Sounds good to me.'

Alex looked down at their clasped hands. She felt inexplicably breathless all of a sudden. She could feel Joe watching her. Then, very deliberately, he turned her hand over and lifted the palm to his lips.

'Very good.'

Her eyes flew to his face. Just for a moment…

But no. He was laughing. Alex tugged her hand away.

'You won't say that when I forget to tell Fran to send your next girlfriend flowers.'

His smile was oddly satisfied. 'But you never do forget.'

'Don't count on it,' said Alex, irritated. 'I have my limits, just like everyone else.'

The smile became enigmatic. 'I'm counting on it.'

She would have demanded that he explain what he meant, but the cab was drawing up outside the office. So, once again, Joe Gomez had the last word. One day, Alex promised herself wistfully, she would turn the tables on him.

But it was not going to be today. When they got back, the incoming messages on her desk resembled the Tower of Pisa. Alex was going to have no more time for verbal duelling with Joe Gomez for several hours. She flung herself into her work with a will.

Joe watched her flicking through the papers. He waited for a moment, then gave a shrug and wandered off to talk to the architects working on the next floor. Alex did not even notice him leave.

He only returned to the office a few hours later, in time to send her home. Alex looked up from an estimate she was checking.

'But…'

'No buts. If I'm taking you out, you need to go home and get ready in good time. I want you looking gorgeous.'

'Well, that could certainly take some time,' she agreed dryly. 'But…'

He leaned over her desk, flipped the laptop computer around to face him, and pressed the 'Save' button.

Alex was half-amused, half-annoyed. 'Who's going to deal with…'

'I will, if necessary.' Joe was impatient. 'I'm not helpless, you know. I did manage to keep a life and a business together before you came aboard.'

Alex blinked. 'Wow. What did I say?'

'All the wrong things,' Joe told her calmly. 'Now, for God's sake, go home and make yourself pretty before I revert to Plan B.'

Alex remembered Plan B. She did not blush at the reminder this time, which had to be a milestone for her.

She locked her drawer. 'I'm gone. I'm gone.'

She found that Joe was holding her coat for her. She let him help her into it, then reached for her briefcase. He took it away from her. 'Seven o'clock,' he said. 'If you're not ready, I shall come in and finish the job.'

'I'll be ready,' Alex vowed.

She was. Slightly uncomfortable in the 1920s dress, she was waiting for him in the sitting room. When Joe rang the bell, she swung her wrap round her shoulders, patted a couple of hairpins back into place and opened the door.

He led her to his silver sports car without commenting on either her promptness or her appearance. Alex told herself she was not piqued. And certainly, when they arrived, he could not have been more attentive. He handed the car keys to a uniformed attendant and put a possessive hand under her elbow.

'Right,' he said. 'Don't let me make any promises – and for God's sake, laugh at all the jokes.'

'Of course,' Alex said composedly. 'After all, I wrote them!'

However, the speech was shorter and funnier than the last time she'd heard it, but basically he'd stuck to her outline. It went down well. Joe received his congratulations modestly, and then urged Alex towards the door.

'Already?' she said, surprised.

'If you don't want me to be reviewing a major city-centre redevelopment,' Joe said blandly.

'*What?*'

'I got talking to a chap from Poland. One moment I was saying they needed to learn from our mistakes. The next...'

Alex groaned.

'It's all right, I didn't give him my business card. If we go now, we can get clean away,' he said in mock-urgent tones.

'Some hopes,' she said.

But she was glad to go. They waited in companionable silence for the car to be brought up from the garage. Another couple was waiting, too. Clearly married. The woman was tired. She leaned against the man with absolute confidence. He put his arm round her protectively.

Alex gave a little shiver. No one had ever held her like that, so publicly, so protectively. So proudly.

She felt her eyes pricking. Tiredness, she told herself, squaring her shoulders.

Joe noticed something was wrong. He looked down at her, cocking an eyebrow. 'Cold?'

'Yes,' Alex said defiantly, although the night was quite unseasonably mild.

'I'll ply you with hot chocolate when I get you home,' he promised. He put his arm round her and gave her a brotherly hug.

Brotherly was good, Alex told herself firmly. Brotherly she could handle. All right, it wasn't proud and protective. But she wasn't writhing on the floor with lust, either. That was progress, surely?

But by the time they got home she was shivering in earnest, in spite of the car's expensive heating. Joe looked at her in concern as he stopped the vehicle. 'You haven't caught a cold, have you?'

'I don't know.' Alex answered, pulling the shawl around her more tightly. 'I walked in the rain this weekend...so maybe.'

He walked her to the door, holding his hand out for her key.

She gave it to him.

'Why on earth did you go walking in the rain?'

There were so many answers to that. All the problems she had to try and sort out: her father...her mother...Rupert. So it was odd that the thing she had kept coming back to, over and over again, was how it felt to be in Joe's arms. And the horrible suspicion that it ought to be like that with Rupert, and that it never would be.

'I had a lot on my mind,' she said coldly.

He let them into the hall, turned on the light and closed the door behind them.

'Then you should talk to me about it. It's silly to brood alone. Even more so to go marching around in weather like this when you don't have to.'

Alex sucked on her teeth and reminded herself that it was pointless to lose her temper.

'I'll remember that.'

He gave a sudden laugh and turned back to her in the narrow hall.

'No, you won't.' He touched her cheek lightly, affectionately. 'You'll do just as you always have – and the hell with good advice from me or anyone else.'

Alex stood as if she had turned to stone. The shivers stopped at the touch of his fingers, and she swallowed audibly.

But Joe did not notice. He was making his way into the kitchen as if the house belonged to him. He went to the fridge.

'Now, that hot drink. Good grief, don't you keep any milk in the house?'

'We're out. I meant to get some on the way home, but I forgot.'

His head came up at that. 'We?'

'I share with Julie,' she reminded him.

'Oh.' He seemed to relax. 'Where is she now?'

Alex looked at her watch. 'At the theatre, I should think. She usually doesn't get in till late.'

'Ah.' He looked round the kitchen. 'Well, no hot chocolate, then. It looks like you've got a straight choice between green tea and brandy.'

'I don't want anything, thank you. I...'

'Yes, you do.'

He took her hands and pressed them together. It was totally unexpected, and as brotherly as the rest of his attitude, but Alex shivered as if someone had tipped a phial of mercury down her spine.

Joe misinterpreted her response. 'There you are. Cold as ice. If you go to bed like that, you'll only get colder and then you won't sleep. I'll make some tea.'

'Th-thank you,' Alex muttered feebly.

He set about the task with a brisk efficiency that widened Alex's eyes. At work he had claimed that he was too incompetent to fill a kettle. She said so.

'Another one of my secrets revealed,' he mourned. 'I'll have to rely on you not to blow my cover.' He looked at her, the wrap still clutched tightly around her. 'Why don't you go into the sitting room and put the fire on?'

She did. After lighting the logs with a whoosh of gas, she sank down beside the fireplace, holding her hands out. Joe was right. She was still exceptionally shaky, though she was not sure that 'cold' was quite the right word to describe her state, she thought wryly. She did not think she was likely to feel any different as long as he stayed, either. So, when he brought in the tea she said, 'Don't feel you have to stay and minister to an invalid. It's only a sniffle, if that.'

He looked faintly annoyed. 'I can afford a civilised half-hour to wind up the evening,' he said firmly.

Maybe, thought Alex. *But can I?*

'Well, that's very kind of you, but...'

Once again he interrupted. 'No, it's not. It's what any man

would want to do after taking a woman out on the town.' He paused, then added mischievously, 'Unless he was taking her to bed, of course.'

Alex bit her lip and said nothing.

Joe helped himself to some brandy and came back to the fire. She thought he would sit in the Queen Anne chair, but he did not. He slipped down onto the rug in front of her and leaned back against the chair, very much at his ease. He looked up at her curiously.

'You really do think you're a complete no-no, don't you, my love?'

'Of course, I don't. I'm stable and competent, and a good deal more reliable than you are,' she said with spirit. 'I'm just not very…'

Over the brandy glass, his expression was unreadable. Was he laughing at her again?

'Very…?' he prompted.

'Well, *attractive*, I suppose. I'm not pretty and feminine and – oh, the sort of woman that men fall in love with.'

The silence was so long that she thought for a moment Joe had fallen asleep. At last he stirred.

'I think you're special,' he said idly.

He was being brotherly again, Alex thought. She hunched her shoulders.

'Sure you do. From your point of view, I'm a good bargain. I know too many of your secrets.'

For a moment, he looked almost angry. 'Not all of them. Don't forget that. I told you.'

She shrugged. 'OK. You're still not a disinterested party.'

He gave a ghost of a laugh. 'Oh, I'm not that, all right.'

She did not understand him and went on, 'You don't see me the same way other men do.'

He put his brandy glass down on the marble fire-surround with a crash that nearly broke it.

'Whose fault is that?' Now he sounded really angry.

Alex stared as he continued, 'Your problem is that you've made yourself invisible.'

He looked at her in blatant challenge, but Alex was too taken aback to rise to it.

'Invisible? I don't understand.'

'Well, you should do. You've no one to blame for it but yourself. You're the one who did it.'

He stood up and began to stride up and down the room. Alex had watched him striding like that around the office for months while he was wrestling with some design problem. Usually she kept silent and let him think out loud, as that was what he wanted. But this was her life he was talking about.

'I haven't done any such thing,' she said indignantly.

He waved her interruption aside as if it were a troublesome fly: annoying, but insignificant. Alex felt her temper start to rise again.

'You should listen to yourself. "I'm not the sort of woman men fall in love with"!' he mimicked savagely. 'It's crazy. If there were only one sort of woman men fall in love with, the human race would have died out before it learned to walk erect on two legs.'

Alex blinked. He sounded as impassioned as he had done this evening when he talked about the future of graceful buildings.

'What you mean is that you've turned yourself into the sort of woman that men don't notice. Or women either, for that matter, unless they've known you all your life,' he added fairly. 'Result: nobody falls in love with you, because nobody sees that you're there to be fallen in love with. I've never met a more deliberately anonymous female in my life. Except at work, of course. You break out of the greyness there, all right.'

'You're very insulting…' Alex began.

'Don't interrupt. I don't know why you do this, and frankly, I don't care. I've been patiently waiting for this nonsense with

Sweetcroft to take its course. But all that happens is that you get more and more convinced that he is a hero, and you are less than the dust beneath his chariot wheels.'

'No,' said Alex faintly.

He took no notice. 'What you ought to do, of course, is return him to the store and get someone a lot more amusing.'

He paused.

Alex was so angry she stopped huddling over the fire. She sat straight up and glared at him. 'Like you would, I suppose.'

'I would never spend five minutes with a woman who made me feel as bad about myself as Rupert Sweetcroft makes you feel all the time,' Joe said frankly.

Alex gasped.

He went on, 'I thought you'd get over it. But it's been going on too long, and you show no signs of standing up for yourself. So, I'm going to take a hand.'

Alex pounded her fist on the seat of the chair. 'How dare you?!' she cried. 'That's my life you're talking about. I...'

'Don't interrupt. Look at the facts. I came back from Mexico to find you sliding down the wall because your boyfriend wouldn't take you to some blasted party.'

That was not the only reason she was sliding down the wall, thought Alex. She considered reminding him of it for a fraught few seconds. Then, just in time, she realised how dangerous it would be. Now was no time to be mentioning office floors, or Venice, or kisses that went a lot further than they were supposed to.

'Now, I accept that there are family tensions there,' Joe continued fair-mindedly, not noticing her reaction. 'But still, why was it such a big deal that he cried off? You're young, attractive and successful. Why can't you walk into this family gathering and tell the whole bunch to treat you with respect or you'll walk out on them?'

Alex stared.

'You see. It hadn't even occurred to you, had it? Don't you

realise, you stupid woman, that you've got the same rights as the rest of the human race? And the same advantages.'

'Yes, of course I do, but…'

'Don't interrupt,' he said for the third time. 'I've been thinking about this all night. And as far as I can see, what you need is a crash course in self-respect. You're a bloody impressive article; you've just got to learn to believe it.'

This was clearly the climax of his speech. He turned on her triumphantly and stood over her, hands on his hips.

Alex felt as if she had been toiling up a slope in the face of a high-velocity wind machine. Now that someone had kindly turned it off, she did not quite know where she was.

'How do you suggest I go about that?' she said at last, at her most reasonable. It was better than screaming at him, though half of her would still have preferred to do just that. She drew a deep breath. 'If you're right – and I'm not saying that you *are*, mind you – but *if* you're right, then by definition I'm going to have trouble believing anything new about myself.'

Joe looked vastly pleased with himself.

'Quite. I also thought about that. What you need is a respray.'

She did not believe her ears. '*What?*'

'A make-over.'

Alex opened her mouth, found that she had no words, and shut it again, shaking her head helplessly.

'Approach it logically,' Joe said in an encouraging tone. 'What is it that makes you feel you're so unattractive to men? You said yourself, you know you're a good bargain once anyone has the sense to see it.'

'That's not quite what I said.'

He waved it away. 'It's what you meant. And you're absolutely right. So why don't the men of your acquaintance see it? Because you don't let them see it.'

'That's not true. I just…'

'Camouflage yourself.' He was beginning to sound positively evangelical, she thought. 'So, we must ask ourselves, what is this disguise that's getting in the way?'

'M-must we?'

'Of course. It's a wicked waste,' he said, coming down off the rostrum for a moment.

She shook her head in confusion. 'Waste of what?'

Joe hunkered down beside her on the rug. He carefully removed the wrap from her fingers where she was clutching it to her breast. Alex did not protest. He spread it open. Then, very gently, he slipped it off her shoulders and down her arms.

One of the thin straps went with it. Alex shivered, though she was not cold at all now.

Joe dropped his head. He seemed to be studying her shoulders. She thought, though she could not be sure, that she felt his mouth against the soft, exposed skin. It was unbelievable. She sat absolutely still.

'A waste of that,' he said softly.

Alex swallowed. There was no sound at all in the room, except for the popping of the gas flames. She knew she ought to do something, say something, and she had no idea what.

Joe straightened. 'It's time someone sorted you out,' he said robustly, breaking the moment so completely that Alex jumped. 'If you won't, I will.'

She scanned his face. She was still half in thrall to that odd moment of tension, but Joe had clearly moved on. *He's serious*, she thought. *It's crazy, but he's actually serious. He must see me as some sort of intellectual puzzle*. The thought was slightly alarming. Joe Gomez loved puzzles.

'You don't need to bother…'

But Joe was too entranced by his idea to listen.

'You're not shy. You were getting on fine with some of the guests this evening,' he told her, revealing that he had been watching her.

'I'm all right if it's about work.' Alex remembered that they had not been talking about work, but about Joe. She flushed and added hurriedly, 'But you're wrong. I am shy. Lavender always says I've got no small talk.'

He was unimpressed. 'Lavender hasn't got anything else. What you need is confidence, not conversation lessons. We can deal with that.'

Alex began to feel alarmed. 'C-can we?'

'Sure. Now, what else makes you feel unattractive?'

Alex bit her lip. But so much of her dignity had been stripped away by Joe's laser analysis of her shortcomings that there was no point in hanging onto the last rag of it.

'I'm plain,' she said brutally.

It was Joe's turn to stare. She smiled ironically. 'That's different from being ugly. You can be quite stylish being ugly. At least people remember you. But I'm just nothing. Grey. You said it yourself.'

He shut his eyes, saying 'God, give me strength.' Then he opened his eyes. 'Don't you ever look in the mirror, you stupid woman?' he said in exasperation.

She gave a wry laugh. 'No more than I have to.'

'You're crazy.' He subjected her to the sort of unimpassioned scrutiny with which he went over every detail of the model of one of his plans. 'You're a good height, nice balance, beautiful shoulders. You stoop sometimes and you shouldn't, but we can take care of that. Good skin. Good cheekbones. Hair needs attention. But the eyes… Good Heavens, Alex, don't you know about your eyes? Men have gone to war and written poems to women with eyes like yours.'

'Wh-what?'

He knelt in front of her.

Alex remembered something Julie had said – about Joe Gomez giving you all his attention. Well, he was certainly giving it all to her now. It was so intense she could have burned up in it. He touched her face so gently that she could hardly feel it – except, of course, that she could feel it through to her heart's core.

'Your eyes are passionate,' he said softly. 'A wonderful colour of dark, velvety brown.'

He stopped. Alex stared, mesmerised by his eloquence. He did not smile, and for a moment he looked almost bitter.

Then he stood up, adding, 'You should dress to match the colour of your eyes,' he told her. 'Make up to emphasise them. Instead of which, you spend your life in boring patterns that would drown even Cleopatra – and you don't seem to wear any make-up at all.'

Alex blinked. This businesslike run-down silenced utterly her.

He seemed to shake off the faint bitterness as he jumped up again, positively crackling with energy. 'Well, that's the diagnosis,' Joe said briskly. 'Now for the remedy.'

Alex was more shaken than she wanted to admit. Some flicker of her normal spirit reasserted itself at last.

'Well, thank you for the consultation,' she said with irony. 'And now I suppose I'm expected to do as I'm told, as usual?'

He looked wounded. 'I'm thinking of your own interests…'

But Alex had worked herself up into a healing rage. She struggled to her feet and faced him. 'You think I'll just do whatever you tell me, and then say "thank you"?' she demanded.

He gave her that beguiling grin again.

'I'm quite certain you wouldn't,' he said frankly. 'That's why I'm taking personal charge of Operation Make-Over.'

chapter nine

To Alex's astonished outrage, Joe began 'Operation Make-Over' first thing the following morning. For once, Alex was still in bed when the phone started ringing. She stayed there, hoping that Julie would answer it. But the phone went on ringing.

Resignedly, she got up, pulled on her robe and trailed out to the kitchen. She propped herself up against the wall and lifted the phone up to her ear.

'Hello?' she said drowsily, suppressing a yawn.

'Make-over alert,' said Joe, sounding disgustingly cheerful. 'I know you haven't woken up yet, but I'm pressed for time. I'll give you half an hour before I'll be round.'

Alex caught herself mid-yawn. 'You can't be serious. It's eight o'clock on a Tuesday morning, and we have work to do.'

'You are so right. We certainly have.'

'But you're seeing the Docklands Development people at twelve,' said Alex, who knew Joe's diary as well as she knew her own.

Joe was unmoved. 'Sure I am. So if we're going shopping, we've got to get moving.'

Alex groped towards understanding. 'Shopping?'

'That's the way we start.'

She passed a hand over her face, trying to wake herself up. 'But I don't *like* shopping.'

'That, my love, is all too obvious. Never mind, I quite enjoy it. In the right circumstances.'

Her bleary eyes caught sight of the wall calendar Julie had pinned up above the phone so they should know each other's movements. She focused on the date and gave a yelp.

'Do you know what day it is?' She counted. 'Two weeks to Christmas Day. No one in their right mind goes shopping in the pre-Christmas frenzy.'

'I do. And you're wasting time. You're down to twenty-five minutes,' he said blithely. 'See you.' And he rang off.

'What? No, don't. Wait. Oh *hell!*' said Alex.

Precisely twenty-five minutes later, Alex opened the door, a little pale but otherwise in control. She was wearing jeans and a jacket over her good, dull lamb's-wool sweater. Joe surveyed the ensemble disapprovingly.

'Don't you have a skirt?' he asked.

Alex was disconcerted. 'What?'

'We're looking for clothes that will make you look and feel wonderful. That means looking at your legs.'

'Oh,' said Alex. She peered at him. 'Is that a compliment?'

'I try,' said Joe, amused. 'No payback yet, but I keep on trying.'

She gave him a fugitive grin. 'Sorry. I must be very unrewarding.'

His eyes did that familiar thing where they went dark, but you sensed that there was a little flame in them.

'I wouldn't say that,' he drawled. 'Go and change. And remember, it has to be something easy to get in and out of.' He looked down at her with a distinctly malicious glint in his eye. 'A lot.'

Alex knew she was being teased, but she was not up to a battle of wills with Joe Gomez so early in the morning.

'I'll change,' she said, resigned.

'Quickly,' he advised. 'I'll keep the cab waiting.'

She growled all the way to Joe's first choice of shop. It turned out to be an outrageously expensive boutique. Alex did not know much about clothes, but she knew that Angelica's House was as exclusive – and expensive – as you could get in London. And that they did not open till nine o'clock.

She said so, triumphantly. 'Noon would be nearer the mark. For the Ladies who Lunch.'

Joe helped her out of the cab and leaned in to pay the driver.

'I rang them. They agreed to open early in the circumstances. And I thought you didn't know anything about shopping!' he said, straightening.

'I have friends. And a grandmother who shops for Britain. This is out of my league.'

'But I like their clothes,' Joe said blandly. He drew her hand through his arm to lead her into the shop.

Alex ground her teeth. 'And that settles it, I suppose?'

'Yup. As long as I'm in charge of the project.'

'*Project…?*'

He held the door open for her, his eyes gleaming. 'This,' he said, 'is going to be fun.'

Alex did not deign to reply.

She only came out of her dignified silence when he brushed aside the elegant suits the assistants were showing her and seized a floor-length, shimmering ruby-coloured, silk-velvet dress.

'Stop showing her uniforms. We want to bring out the hidden Alex. Try that.'

'It's indecent!' Alex yelped, taking in the neckline with a blink.

Joe took no notice. 'Ruby,' he said, concentrating. 'With your skin and hair, you should always wear jewel colours. Go and try it on.'

Urged on by assistants who seemed to know him suspiciously well, Alex went.

'It's refreshing to see a husband taking such an interest,' said the older assistant chattily.

Alex jumped. 'We're not married,' she protested. 'He's my business partner.'

The older woman smiled. 'In my day, only a husband

would be so possessive.'

Alex was disconcerted. A *husband*? Joe?

She had never thought of Joe marrying anyone, she realised. Affairs, yes. But marriage? Not the Joe she knew. But could there be another Joe she did not know?

She was so distracted by the idea that she let them zip her into the dress he had chosen. She even let them whisk away her bra with only a token protest. They gave the dress a final pat and propelled her out into the salon.

'There,' said the older assistant proudly.

Joe stood up slowly.

Alex did not want to meet his eyes. Instead, she turned away – and caught sight of herself in the long mirror at the end of the room. At least, she supposed it was herself. She would never have been sure, if it hadn't been for the floor-length ruby velvet.

She looked at the little figure in the mirror wonderingly.

Suddenly, she was not short, she was delicate. Not round, but voluptuous. Not pallid, but luminous. She was a stranger. A beautiful stranger.

Beautiful? Impossible!

She took two cautious steps forward, unaware that everyone had fallen silent, watching her.

She ran a hand very gently down the pile of the silk-velvet dress. It felt alive, almost as if it was breathing with her. She could feel the stuff mould itself to the swell of her breasts as they rose and fell, first cool, then warm as fire. Her shadowed skin in the deep cleavage was moon-pale. Even her tangle of hair had somehow metamorphosed into a scented mass a man could bury his face in....

Very slowly, she raised one arm to hold her hair on top of her head. The dress slid over her skin like water. Her ears, her throat, her nape were an elegant curve, painted by a lover of beauty, exquisite. Alex gave a deep, deep sigh.

'Yes,' Joe said softly.

He was standing behind her. Close. She met his eyes in the mirror.

Alex did not know if he was going to touch her. She only knew she wanted him to. Wanted him to so fiercely that it hurt. She even felt herself sway backwards towards him...

And then one of the women drew a long, delighted breath, and she broke out of the dream. As quick as lightning, Alex retreated to the end of the shop.

'What else should I try on?' she asked the assistants, trying to get her breath back under some sort of control.

They showed her the rail of clothes that Joe had picked out.

There was crisp cotton, darkly shadowed velvet, silk that ran through the fingers like water. There were slim dresses, swirling evening dresses, cocktail dresses, beaded and embroidered dresses. There were severe suits for business, and fantasy suits for the party of a lifetime. There were structured work clothes, loose and comfortable casual clothes, and clothes of such startling sophistication that Alex barely recognised herself when she put them on. But, in colours ranging from midnight sapphire to blood-red ruby, they could all have come out of a jeweller's window.

'Don't tell me,' she said, surveying a knee-length amethyst confection, misted over with floating georgette scarves, and an evening dress in topaz brocade. 'Jewel colours, huh?'

'Good to know you listen to me sometimes,' Joe murmured.

The assistant beamed.

Oh God, she'll think he's being possessive again, thought Alex in an agony of embarrassment. *A possessive husband!*

That was crazy, of course. It was about as likely as the moon being made of finest old Stilton, Alex thought. But just for a moment, under the influence of the assistant's romantic bias, she could almost dream that the man who stood behind her, watching her in the mirror, could be the man her heart turned to.

But Joe Gomez was a red-hot lover, and she was a one-man woman with terminal cold feet. And her one man was Rupert Sweetcroft. Or was he?

She shivered. Whoever Joe married – if he married anyone – was none of her business, she told herself. Not in real life. And dreams were dangerous.

So, she concentrated on the job in hand.

'Have you made your choice?' the assistant asked eventually.

Alex began to answer, 'I'll need to think about it...'

'Yes, she's made her choice,' said Joe. He pointed to the suits and dresses that Alex had particularly liked. 'And don't forget the ruby velvet,' he added, giving them Alex's address so the clothes could be sent on later.

Alex went to change back into her clothes. She tried hard not to think of it as hiding in the broom cupboard, but she had to blow her nose hard several times before she climbed back into her old navy skirt.

The older assistant came in to collect the topaz evening gown, and to tidy away the rejected clothes. She helped Alex shrug herself back into her jacket, then straightened it in some way that made it indefinably smarter, simultaneously fluffing her unruly mop out along its severe shoulders.

'Thank you,' said Alex, subdued.

The woman gave her a little pat on the shoulder. It was clearly meant as encouragement.

'He is clearly a man who knows his own mind. It wouldn't be easy to refuse him once he had decided on something.' It sounded almost like a warning.

Alex gave an uneasy laugh. 'Oh, we can usually reach a compromise.'

But there was not much compromise about the rest of that whirlwind morning.

'Shoes,' said Joe, hailing a taxi as they left the shop. Sitting in the cab, he brought out his personal organiser, frowning over some notes. 'Gloves. Bags. Underwear.'

'*Underwear?*' echoed Alex, startled.

'If you're going to look gorgeous, you've got to feel gorgeous. Then you go out and see how Rupert Sweetcroft likes you when you feel good about yourself.'

Alex stiffened.

'After that, you can make your own mind up.' He gave a sudden low chuckle. 'I hope. Main object throughout – your happiness!' And he waved his hands like a magician revealing a successful illusion.

Alex said dryly, 'You're forgetting one thing. My happiness doesn't usually depend on what I'm wearing. Most of the time, I forget it as soon as I've got it on.'

'Quite. And no one's been taking it off, as a result,' said Joe outrageously.

Alex glared. 'If you're trying to make me blush, forget it.'

'Aw, shucks. You're no fun any more.'

She grinned, in spite of herself. 'Much more of this, and I'll have complete immunity,' she told him.

Joe did not laugh, though. His eyes seemed to darken.

'Then I'll have to change my tactics,' he said softly.

'Nice try,' said Alex coolly. 'Still no blush. Go on, feel. Cool as a cucumber.'

And she took his hand to her cheek.

A mistake. More of a mistake than she could ever have imagined. One moment she was laughing at him, giving as good as she got. In control. The next… the next…

He stroked her cheek. That was it. Nothing more. Just that. But it felt as if he was saying, 'You're mine.'

It was unexpected. It was unlikely as hell. It was unreconstructed, primitive possessiveness. And she responded to it with unreconstructed, primitive desire.

Cool as a cucumber? Not in a million years.

One-man woman? Whatever happened to that old idea?

Alex held her breath as her whole world fell apart.

With a sigh, Joe took his hand away, and glanced down at his watch.

What followed was, as she told him, like a fantasy-fairground ride. He did not take her to any more exclusive dress shops. Instead, he whisked her in and out of so many boutiques, shoe shops, lingerie departments and perfumeries that her head began to spin. Eventually, they came out of a Mayfair shoe shop and she stopped dead on the pavement,

'Enough!'

Joe was hailing another taxi. He looked over his shoulder. 'What is it?'

'I said, I've had enough. My sinuses hurt with all the perfume I've been sniffing, and I've seen so much lace I can't tell a teddy from a handkerchief.'

He came back to her. 'That will come,' he said with a chuckle. 'When you get used to the idea. For the moment, you're suffering from culture shock.' He sounded pleased.

Alex looked at him, hot-eyed. 'It's all very well for you. You go off to your meeting and forget all of this. I've got to go home tonight and unpack it all when it's delivered. Then I've got to *wear* it.'

'That's the idea,' he agreed gravely.

She shook her head. 'I shan't feel like myself at all. I don't even feel like myself now.' She was only half joking.

'Small period of adjustment,' said Joe, without sympathy. 'You'll get used to it.'

'Will I?' She sounded mournful.

'Yes, you will. And when you do, you will enjoy it,' he said firmly. He bent and gave her a quick, light kiss on the mouth. Alex's pulse flew round the clock and settled back again to double speed.

To disguise it, she said teasingly, 'Do you trust me to go to the hairdressers on my own?'

He touched her face. 'Just don't let them do anything too

crazy. I like you wild and curly. I'd miss it.'

Alex was still trying to get her breath back when he breezed off. It was, in lots of ways, a relief. But there was still a desolate little clutch at her heart as she watched him drive on in yet another cab to his meeting. He did not look back.

For the first time in her life, she did not go back to the office as she normally would. Instead, she went home. But she was still conscientious enough to call in and check that there were no emergencies.

'Don't worry,' Fran told her blithely. 'Joe said you were taking the day off. We're coping fine.'

'Oh,' said Alex, not sure whether she was entirely pleased about that.

But there were a lot of things that needed thinking about, let alone the clothes that needed trying on again. She put the phone down and went to the bathroom to draw a long, scented bath.

Then she took off her clothes and sank back in its warmth, sniffing appreciatively as the Roman oils filled the steamy bathroom. It was only as she slipped under the softened water that she realised how stiff her shoulders must have been.

Blast Joe for getting her so stewed up. Ruby velvet! Silk underwear! Italian perfume!

'I don't like feeling like a project,' she told herself, speaking aloud in her bath. *You didn't feel like a project when he kissed you*, a small voice reminded her, *you felt like a woman for the first time in your life.*

'Anyone would,' she told the small voice stoutly. 'He kisses like a dream.'

And has a body to die for, the inner voice said smugly.

Alex shifted her shoulders uncomfortably. 'Well, of course he has,' she told the voice. 'Even Julie was drooling over him – and Julie has worked with some first-class male crumpet in her time. It's not surprising that someone like me would turn into a warm puddle of lust, now, is it?'

And he stroked your cheek as if he loved you.

Alex sat up abruptly, sending scented water sloshing wildly.

'Joe Gomez is a cool customer with a swathe of broken hearts behind him,' she announced to the steamy walls. 'He's got to be good at it. Don't get carried away here.'

She climbed out of the bath and wrapped the warm, fluffy towel around here as if it was a parka and she was on an Arctic ice floe.

She peered in the mirror. She was a lot more flushed than the steam justified.

'You'd better stay a project,' she advised her newly moisturised face with feeling. 'It's safer.'

So when, the next day, Julie commented on the number of carrier bags and wondered aloud at the reason for Joe's involvement, Alex was strictly non-committal.

'Decided he wants to improve the office décor, has he?' speculated Julie, one shrewd eyebrow cocked at a glossy purple shoebox. 'I suppose he's tired of having his office run by Joan of Arc. I don't blame him.'

'What do you mean, *Joan of Arc*?'

'Work it out,' said Julie, on her way out. She put her head back around the door. 'I hope this means we'll be seeing the end of Rupert, by the way. Joe's so much more decorative,' she added with a grin, whisking herself away with a laugh before Alex could throw things.

But Alex did not feel like throwing things. She knew Julie was teasing her. And she was fairly sure that Joe was teasing her, too.

Yet for Alex, it all felt frighteningly real, no matter how much good advice she gave herself. No matter how much she knew that Joe was out of her league. And no matter how much she knew told herself that, for him, 'Project Make-Over' was no more than an amusing challenge.

If she had needed any further evidence of that fact, she got it the following morning when Joe called a meeting. He ran through the work in hand, his appointments for the rest of the week and two new jobs for which they been asked to tender. Then he put down his scribbled list, put his feet up on the desk and made a public announcement of intent.

'Alex has turned over a new leaf,' he told their assembled colleagues. 'From now, I am in charge of her appearance. As a start, anyone seeing her in tartan is responsible for tearing it off her back.'

There was a stunned silence.

'That's all,' said Joe, as matter-of-fact as if he had just announced a small décor change. Which, thought Alex, reluctantly amused, she supposed he had.

When they had all filed out, Alex sat on the corner of her desk, sipping cold coffee and watching him. 'Was that really necessary?' she asked at last.

He was flicking his papers into rapid order. At her question, he did not look up from the task, even briefly.

'Mmm?'

'Announcing "Operation Make-Over" on the public address system,' Alex elaborated, her tone dry.

'Oh, that.' Frowning, he fished out a slim blue folder and put it on top of the pile. 'Yes, I think so.'

He said no more. She swung her legs, waiting for him to go on. He stood behind his desk, his eyes skimming the first page in the blue folder in front of him, and his frown deepened. Alex drummed her heels.

'Would you care to explain?' she invited him sweetly.

He looked up then, his expression absent. 'Explain? Explain what?'

She kept cool. 'Why you have just made a present of my private life to our entire workforce,' she said with restraint.

'Oh. That.'

'Yes. That.'

He flicked the folder shut. 'Well, it's not going to be very private, is it?'

'I don't see why.'

Joe looked amused. 'For one thing, in this office you and I are the bosses. What the bosses do gets talked about.'

'Rubbish! No one notices what I wear.'

'Transformation, they'll notice,' Joe said dryly.

Alex shifted her shoulders irritably. 'Even so…'

He looked impatient, and suddenly rather remote. 'Gossip is everywhere. If we don't tell, people are going to smell it out.'

She was bewildered. 'Smell what out?'

'That you and I are seeing more of each other than we ever have before.' He was sardonic. 'Believe me, Alex, there's only one way to deal with gossip like that. Head it off before people think they have uncovered a secret.'

She stared.

'We're going to see a lot of each other. Fine. We tell everyone in advance. So when Alasdair sees you in my car at two in the morning, he won't think he's found out some great secret that he has just got to tell Fran, who will just have to tell Reg, who will… get the picture?'

She said slowly, 'They'll think we're having an affair.'

He shrugged. 'I imagine so.'

'I never thought of that.'

His face hardened. 'Worried what Sweetcroft will think?'

She shook her head, slowly.

'No.'

No, I'm not worried what Rupert will think. I'm worried about what I'm thinking right now.

I'm thinking: I want to have an affair with you. I don't care how short it is, or how hurt I am when it's over.

I want to be touched as if I'm loved, even if it's only for a little while. I want to feel – and the hell with whether I can cope or not. I want a red hot lover.

I want you.

chapter ten

'Oh lord,' Alex said aloud.

Joe frowned. 'He'll get used to it.'

Alex shook her head, not attending. 'What price loyalty? What price love?' she asked herself.

She had loved Rupert all her life. She had *promised* him. She always kept her promises. Always. She knew what happened when people didn't. She had seen it with her parents. She had vowed that she would never let anyone down like that. Up to now, she never had.

Up to now? What was she thinking of? Joe, that's what.

It was just as well that Fran chose that moment to put her head round the door. Otherwise, Alex thought, she would have sat there staring at Joe like some mesmerised woodland animal.

Fran, however, was impervious to the atmosphere.

'Your grandmother's been on the phone,' she told Alex. 'She's on her way with your Christmas present. She said she wanted to surprise you. But I thought you'd fancy a bit of notice.'

'Thank you,' said Alex with genuine gratitude. 'I'll freshen up.'

She tidied her smart new haircut in the cloakroom. Joe had not commented on it, but Alex liked it more and more. It was shaped to reveal her high cheekbones, making her brow look wide and clear, her eyes deep. It was a small difference, and yet it seemed as if it had somehow made her less other people's right-hand person, and more herself.

'Heaven knows what will happen to me when I step into the topaz brocade,' Alex told her reflection with a grin. It was a shaky grin, but at least it was a move in the right direction.

She went back to the office. Joe was standing with his back to the window. He looked unusually forbidding.

Alex was instantly nervous. According to her grandmother, Joe had said unforgivable things to her the last time they met. *Please don't let them have a row*, she prayed. *I don't think I could bear it.*

Aloud, she said in her most prosaic tone, 'She won't stay long.'

He frowned. 'Why is she bringing your present here?'

'I don't really know. Perhaps she was in the area.'

He dismissed it with an impatient flick of the hand. 'Aren't you spending Christmas with her?'

'Oh,' said Alex. She looked at her toes. 'Er... no.'

'Why not?' His voice was unexpectedly harsh.

Alex looked up. 'She's going on a cruise with a friend. She's always wanted to. I think it's a good idea. This weather is so bad for her rheumatism.'

'*She's* going away?'

'Yes, I told you. Madeira and points east.'

'Not you?'

'Me?' Alex jumped.

'It's a reasonable question. Don't you spend Christmas with her, normally?'

She sat at her desk and started to play with the contents of her penholder.

'Mmm. Slightly difficult area.'

'Why?' He shot it at her like an arrow.

Alex blinked. She looked up at him, puzzled. He was not usually so interested in where she spent her free time. She told him the truth. 'Well – my mother is probably going to the health farm, like she usually does. Daughters are not required. My father wants me to go to his house, my stepmother doesn't. Although, she hasn't actually said so, of course.'

Joe relaxed visibly. 'So? What will you do?'

Alex pursed her lips. 'I don't know yet.'

'It's less than a fortnight away.'

'Thank you,' Alex said with irony. 'I was almost forgetting.'

He laughed. 'Maybe I have a suggestion.'

But the door was flung back and he had no time to expand on his idea, whatever it was. Lavender Eyre had been dramatic all her life, and could never come into a room without making an entrance. Fran followed behind, bearing her packages.

'Darling.' Lavender embraced Alex, scattering pens and pencils without noticing. 'You've done something to your hair. How nice.'

'Thank you,' murmured Alex in response.

Over her grandmother's shoulder, she could see Joe grinning. She indicated him. Her grandmother turned to look at Joe coldly.

'Ah. Dear boy,' Lavender said, employing a frosty tone. 'How are you treating my Alex, now that you've succeeded in poaching her?'

'With all the love and care that such a jewel deserves,' said Joe promptly. 'Just like you didn't!'

He set a chair for Lavender, though.

'How are you?' he asked solicitously. He thought she was a hypochondriac, and did not make a secret of it. 'Rheumatism thriving?'

Lavender glared. 'I am well. I want a word with my granddaughter.'

Joe shrugged. 'Fine. I'll be in the butler's pantry.'

He went. Alex choked, and then did her best to rearrange her features to a suitably enquiring expression. It was not very successful.

'That young man has a regrettable idea of what is funny,' Lavender told her. 'Anyone would think I was a snob.'

Alex chuckled. 'Ah come on, Grandma. Your best friend wouldn't call you a practising democrat.'

'You're letting him influence you.' It was an accusation.

'Yes,' agreed Alex, amused. She was glad that her grandmother did not know the full details of just how right she was. 'Yes, I'd have to own up to that.'

'You'd better take care. But never mind that now. I've had a letter from your Trustees.'

'I thought you might,' agreed Alex.

'They say you don't object to them making a payment to your father. Is that true?'

'Yes, quite right,' said Alex gently. 'I don't object.'

Lavender's eyes filled unexpectedly. 'When your grandfather set up that trust, he meant it to be for their marriage, their children. Not… not this, this travesty of a family celebration.'

'I know,' said Alex, her heart wrung. Lavender did not cry easily. 'But things change.'

Lavender made a gallant attempt to pull herself together.

'No use crying over spilt milk.' She tilted her chin. 'I won't have the Trust paying out to keep that hussy in mink. Or that daughter of hers, either. I suppose we'll have to do something about your father's house if the roof really *is* falling off.'

Alex said gently, 'That's what I told Mr Rengo. If you agree, he can go ahead.'

Lavender sat very straight. 'Just the repair bills. They can be sent direct to Rengo's office. I'm not letting your father have any money, or That Woman will get her hands on it.'

Alex bit her lip. 'They've been married for ten years.'

'And he was married to your mother for twenty. He should never have let himself be trapped.'

'Surely it's up to him?'

'It ruined your mother's life. People should keep their word.'

Alex looked away. That hurt.

'And I'm not releasing any money for him to give that girl a Season. She ought to get herself some training and go and find a job.'

Alex was glum. She had not expected much else, but it was still lowering to hear how vindictive her grandmother still was after all these years.

'It's not Laine's fault that our father behaved badly…'

'Maybe not. But I hear she is a complete minx,' said Lavender, whose information network would have made the CIA envious. She got up and shook out her smart tweed coat. 'Don't try and sell any of your sweet forgiveness to me, my girl. I'm far too old to give up a good grudge.'

Alex stood up and hugged her. 'All right. No comment.' She walked to the office door with her. 'Have a lovely holiday.'

Lavender returned the hug. 'Hope the dance isn't too vile. Though I suppose at your age, any dance is fun, and Rupert will be there, after all. He wouldn't have been my choice for you, but once you make up your mind, you're a faithful little thing.' She patted Alex's cheek with unusual warmth. 'Better get him to propose while you're at it. It's about time I danced at your wedding.'

Ouch. This time the hurt went right to the heart.

'Yes,' said Alex colourlessly.

Lavender left, and Joe strolled back into the office.

'What has she given you?'

Alex looked at the brightly coloured parcel. It was large and octagonal. She knew that shape.

'One of the new gift caskets. I only hope she never finds out that I had a facial at a salon that doesn't use her products,' she said with feeling.

'Poor Alex. Your loyalty is taking a real hammering, isn't it?'

'Oh hell,' said Alex with repressed fury. 'Why does everyone have to keep telling me how faithful and loyal I am? I'm only human.'

Joe stared.

She subsided. 'Sorry. Family stuff. Always rubs me up the wrong way.'

'I can see it does.' Joe hesitated, then said abruptly, 'I suppose Lavender approves of Rupert Sweetcroft?'

Alex was startled. 'What?'

'She said she wanted to dance at your wedding.'

'You were listening at the door!' she accused.

He was shameless. 'Of course. Does she?'

Alex shook her head. 'No. She barely knows him. It's just that my grandmother thinks every woman ought to be married. It's her generation.'

'And class,' Joe added swiftly.

Alex sighed. 'You've got a real hang-up about her being "upper class".'

He was affronted. 'No more than she has. When we set up the partnership she rang me, you know. Said you and I could never work together. We came from such different backgrounds we were completely incompatible.'

'So she was wrong,' said Alex with a shrug. 'So what?'

For a moment, his mouth twisted. 'Was she?'

'Of course.' Alex was impatient. 'Can you imagine working this harmoniously with anyone else? I can't.'

He looked out of the window. 'Maybe that's the problem.'

She did not understand him, so said nothing. After a moment, he turned back to her.

'So you're spending Christmas in cosy domesticity with Sweetcroft? Or are you off skiing?'

Alex winced. She pulled a file towards her. 'Neither,' she said crisply.

Joe waited. She said nothing more.

'OK. What *are* you doing for Christmas?' he demanded.

Cornered, Alex sent him a look of dislike. 'It's none of your business. Aren't I allowed any private life at all? I promise,' she added waspishly, 'that whatever I'm doing, I won't wear tartan.'

There was a sharp silence. Then he began to laugh, at first softly, then throwing back his head and filling the tall room with the sound. Alex glared.

'Harmony,' said Joe, when he could speak. 'Lord bless us, some harmony. What would a full-scale fight be like?'

But he went about the rest of the day whistling.

He might be cheerful, but Alex was feeling worse and worse. By the time she went home, she was ready to confess everything to Rupert and throw herself on his mercy.

It was crazy. She had never thought of herself as fickle. Hell, she had been faithful to Rupert her whole life. How could she have turned into this feral creature that stalked Joe Gomez with her eyes when he was there, and thought about him all the time when he wasn't? She even dreamed about him, for God's sake. Alex was rapidly coming to the conclusion that she no longer knew herself.

Rupert had been her only lover. She had never wanted anyone else. She had gone out with other men, of course, but she had always made it plain that she was not available. And they respected it. She had not even found it difficult.

And now she only had to look across at Joe, and she broke out into a cold sweat of longing. If he pushed his hair out of his eyes... or ran those long, sensitive fingers through his hair...or stretched his arms above his head so she saw the play of muscles under his shirt...

'Get a grip,' Alex told herself feverishly. 'Get a grip.'

She had to call Rupert. Yes, that would steady her. She knew the New York hotel where he usually stayed. She would call as soon as she thought he would be back.

She tried. Rupert was checked in all right, the desk clerk assured her, but he was not answering his phone. Maybe she could try again later.

She did – all through the evening. But he did not come back, and in the end she went to bed. She slept fitfully, fighting off dreams of men who beckoned and had dark, wicked eyes.

Eventually, she got up and looked at her bedside clock.

Midnight in New York, she thought – that was not too late to call. Rupert was a night owl.

She padded out to the kitchen, huddling her old dressing gown around her, and dialled.

Once again, the hotel telephonist connected her, but the telephone rang and rang. She was on the point of hanging up when the phone was picked up at last.

'Hello,' said a voice.

Alex froze. It was not Rupert. It was a girl – a distinctly sleepy girl, with an oddly familiar voice.

'I'm sorry. I think I must have the wrong number,' she stammered.

'Do you want Rupert? Hang on, he's just coming.'

Rupert! It wasn't a wrong number, after all. Alex felt numb. She did not say anything. She couldn't.

'Hello? Rupert Sweetcroft here.'

Yes, it was unmistakably Rupert. He did not sound asleep, at least. He sounded exactly as Alex knew him: impatient, hectoring, on the edge of annoyance. She opened her mouth to speak, but no sound came out.

'Hello?' Rupert was getting annoyed. 'Laine, are you sure there was someone on the line? All I can hear is a lot of crackle.'

Laine? *Laine?*

The girl gave a sleepy giggle. 'Well, I was asleep, darling. But I thought it rang. That's what woke me.'

There were kissing sounds that made Alex feel slightly sick.

'And now I'm awake…' murmured the girl.

Her intention was clear. Alex could almost see her reaching for him.

She flung the phone down as if it had gone nuclear.

Laine! Rupert must have taken her with him on his business trip. And he was now making love to her.

All of a sudden, a lot of things fell into place.

He had found it so easy to cool the relationship. And he had lost interest in making love to her for weeks before that. No, not weeks, thought Alex, flaying herself with memory. Months. In fact, he had never really been interested unless she was reluctant. Then it became some sort of challenge, and he seemed to get a buzz out of it.

She dropped her head in her hands. All those sessions of slightly suffocating discomfort. All those hours lying beside him in the dark, after he had fallen asleep, feeling bruised and lonely. He had said she was frigid. But he had been angry, and afterwards he had apologised. He had not meant it, he'd said. But it was Alex who had wondered if it was true. And went on wondering.

Listening to Laine as she wooed Rupert back to bed with enthusiasm, Alex had a revelation. She had never cooed at Rupert like that. Never wanted to.

'Oh, God…I really must be frigid,' she whispered.

But Rupert was still a faithless bastard, and she was not losing sight of that. Because another thing that had fallen into place was his reluctance to take her to Laine's dance.

Now it all made horrible sense. It wasn't that he had forgotten the date. It wasn't even that the job was too important for him to postpone that trip. Or that his private life couldn't be allowed to interfere with his work. It was his private life that was running the show. He just hadn't had the courage to tell Alex.

Alex's anger turned into a slow burn.

She had only been dreaming of Joe Gomez, and she had felt disloyal. She had been going to pour it all out to Rupert. Ask for his help. Ask his forgiveness, for Heaven's sake.

Forgiveness!

'I'll cut his liver out,' hissed gentle, reasonable Alex, gentle and reasonable no longer. 'I'll boil him in oil. I'll get my own back if it's the last thing I do.'

It did not last, of course. By the time she had to get ready for work in the morning, she was back seeing things from Rupert's point of view again.

She knew all the arguments. She had been working too hard. She was too involved with her family. She had not spent enough time with Rupert. She had taken him for granted. She had even been comparing him in her head with Joe. That had to be unfair. Everyone was telling her that Joe Gomez was a world-class Sex Object. No ordinary man could stand up to a rival like that. It was not entirely Rupert's fault.

But still, he should have told her.

And why did it have to be Laine?

She was quiet at work. Joe was out most of the day, so nobody noticed. He breezed in briefly, demanded directions to her father's house and a timetable for Saturday, and breezed out again, without noticing anything was wrong. In fact, when she thought about it, he was still whistling.

She worked later, went home reluctantly and was in as soon as she decently could be the next day. She photocopied a map and put it together with the stiff invitation card on his desk.

'You really don't want to go to that dance in the country, do you?' Fran asked Alex when she went out to the main office to get some coffee. 'Cheer up! The Christmas party is next week. Now that's going to be *seriously* wild. Just as well to get some training in.'

Alex smiled, but inwardly she was wincing. What a prim, buttoned-up idiot they must think her. What a prim, buttoned-up idiot she was! Rupert had a lot of reasons for doing what he did.

It didn't make her feel any better.

She went to her make-up lesson and took such grim notes that the beautician decided she had to be some journalist doing an anonymous test, and gave her twice the attention she normally would.

Alex emerged with huge eyes and full, sensual mouth. The face in the mirror startled her. She did not think she wanted to take it back to the office; that would *really* start them talking.

So, for the second time in a week she went home early.

Julie looked up from the fire, where she was reading a magazine before going to the theatre, and gasped when she saw Alex.

'You look sensational!'

Alex unbuttoned her raincoat with vicious little jabs. 'I look like a Venetian courtesan,' she said with furious precision as she stamped off to her room. 'It's a complete sham.'

But she couldn't resist looking at herself in the mirror. All right, it *was* artifice. It would come off with cleanser, and God knows whether her notes would be good enough for her to recreate the look tomorrow. But this evening Julie was right; she *did* look sensational.

She touched shy fingers to the voluptuously scarlet mouth, and remembered Joe saying, 'Your mouth will get you into trouble. It's too passionate.'

She had dismissed it as teasing then. Passionate? Dull and moderate Alex Eyre, *passionate*? That had to be nonsense. She had certainly never seen any sign of passion in herself.

Well, not then. Now, though…

Alex leaned into the mirror, searching her face for the woman she seemed to be turning into. The woman that Joe had seen all those months ago.

Joe… Her lips parted. And suddenly, the woman in the mirror was not a Venetian courtesan anymore; she was a woman in love, dreaming of her lover.

Alex shut her eyes. 'Fantasy,' she said aloud, fiercely.

So when Joe rang, she was polite, but cool.

'I was wondering whether you really wanted to come to this dance tomorrow,' she said crisply.

'Cold feet, huh?' said Joe. He did not sound surprised, thought Alex, annoyed.

'Not at all. But Rupert was right. I'm not a child. I could go on my own perfectly well. No need to ruin your weekend. We won't get back to London till breakfast.'

'I've thought of that.' Joe sounded pleased with himself. 'I've booked us a room.'

All Alex's phoney coolness evaporated. She gulped and could not speak.

'Hello? You still there?'

Alex massaged her throat. 'Yes,' she managed to croak.

'Well, I thought about it. I know you don't care about clothes that much. But you'll have more fun if you can get ready and go straight to the dance. A couple of hours in the car and your skirts would be crushed to hell. And you'd be thoroughly on edge by the time we got there. A room in the local pub seemed the answer.'

Alex massaged her throat some more.

'A room? *A* room? As in, one between us?'

Joe was resigned. 'Don't give me a hard time, Alex. It was hard enough to find one. Your stepsister seems to have cornered the market for her friends.'

Alex could believe that. The prospect of sharing a room with him filled her with misgiving, but she could not blame him for that, in all fairness. She was the one who had the problem with ungovernable fantasies. Joe was only trying to be helpful. She said in a strangled voice, 'It's very good of you to bother.'

He said lightly, 'You don't think so now. But believe me, you will tomorrow. I'll pick you up in good time.'

So she ended up packing a weekend case and putting her topaz dress in its protective cover.

'This dance is definitely beginning to look up,' pronounced Julie. 'It's about time you got yourself a replacement boyfriend.'

'He's not a boyfriend,' said Alex wearily. She needed to keep reminding herself of it, but it was no fun having to repeat it for Julie's benefit. 'Joe is taking me to Laine's dance because he said I needed support. But that's where it ends.'

'You get tipped out of the coach at midnight?' Julie sounded distinctly sceptical.

'No, of course not.'

'So he's bringing you back to London?'

'Well…' Alex realised suddenly that she could not let Julie leave the door unlocked all night, since she knew she would be spending the night in Suffolk. Besides, if her friend got up on Sunday morning and found that Alex was not there, she'd probably call the police.

She cleared her throat and said as airily as she could manage, 'Actually, Joe decided it was more practical to spend the rest of the night down there.'

'Oh?'

'He will bring me back, but not until Sunday morning.'

Julie pursed her lips, and Alex braced herself for the inevitable taunt. Yet all her friend said was, 'Good idea. He's a real forward-planner, isn't he? Good man, your Joe.'

'He's not *my* Joe,' said Alex. It was becoming a mantra.

She saw that Julie was laughing at her openly. Alex shook her head, but she could not resist smiling. 'And you can stop looking like that. It's all in your imagination.'

'Oh, not just mine,' drawled Julie. 'Not from the sound of it.'

But it is, thought Alex, sadly, *it is*. Oh, Joe teased her. He laughed at her. He respected her. He trusted her with his business, and he sometimes even took her advice on clients. But he was not in love with her. He was a sexy man who appreciated women. He just didn't realise, thought Alex, the effect that sort of appreciation could have on someone who wasn't used to it.

And anyway, she wasn't thinking clearly at the moment. Ever since she had heard Laine answer Rupert's telephone, her head and her heart seemed to have disconnected. Some of the time she hardly seemed to care at all, but sometimes she felt so betrayed she could hardly bear the pain.

Hell, maybe I'm still in love with Rupert after all.

But that was hardly likely. She remembered one of Lavender's favourite sayings: 'Fool me once, shame on you. Fool me twice, shame on me.'

No, she wasn't standing in line for Rupert to make a fool of her for a second time, Alex promised herself. But that was no reason why she should ask another man to pick up the baton, she thought savagely. It would be quite nice not to be any man's fool for a bit.

And yet Joe had never tried to make a fool of her. Oh, he had kissed her, sure. But he had not told her any lies, or offered her any false hope.

Alex thrust her hands up through her hair to still her whirling brain.

The only thing I'm sure of is that I'm not sure of anything.

But she was pretty sure the feelings she had for Joe were temporary. She was not the sort of woman to fall headlong in love. Not even with his dark, gypsy eyes and the sort of intensity that could make your head swim.

But she was an intelligent woman. She had masterly self-control. She never acted rashly, and always thought hard before making any move. All she had to do was to hang onto the habits of a lifetime to help her keep her secret, and she would get through this weekend with her dignity intact. How hard could that be?

Even so, thought Alex, as the doorbell rang and her pulse went into overdrive, *the sooner I get over this madness, the better*.

She opened the door cautiously. The big silver sports car was double-parked in the mews immediately outside her door. The rain was falling in sheets. Joe had his collar up, his dark hair plastered to his head, and he was laughing.

*Oh God, I want you,*she thought, before she could stop herself. Alex was sure it was written on her face. She felt naked.

But Joe was shaking the rain out of his eyes. By the time he was seeing clearly again, she was in control of herself. With a bit of luck, he would not have noticed. It was only for one tiny moment. Maybe she was safe – maybe.

But with a response level like that, keeping her secret safe was going to be a full-time job, Alex thought, her heart sinking even further.

Joe picked up the overnight case she had left by the door. 'Ready?'

No, thought Alex.

But aloud she said, with a self-mockery she hoped he would never know about, 'Ready as I'll ever be.'

chapter eleven

Joe took the dress bag from her and laid it out carefully on top of the cases in the boot. Then he handed her into the Jensen with a quaint air of ceremony.

'Trying to make me feel like Cinderella?' Alex teased him, feeling just a little breathless.

'Just trying to spoil you a little,' he corrected.

There was a caressing note in his voice. Oh that voice! He probably did not even know he was doing it, Alex thought. She was torn between amusement and despair. He just did it automatically to any woman he met. And the ones he spoiled – how she hated the idea – even for a little while had to think themselves lucky. She said repressively, 'So where are we staying?'

'A mediaeval coaching inn. Called 'The Fox'. Claims to have antique furniture.'

'Very efficient,' she commented.

'I don't need you to make all my arrangements for me, my love.'

She swallowed. 'No, I imagine you can handle a weekend for two admirably.'

It sounded waspish, and she did not mean it to. Alex could have kicked herself.

Even more so when he glanced sideways and said, 'Jealous? You've no reason.'

'I know,' she said in a low voice.

Of course, she had no reason to be jealous of Joe's usual weekend companions. He had chosen them, whereas he had just been stuck with her.

She sat on the thought hard. She could not afford to think

like that – or to let him talk too personally. A couple of hours in this luxuriously warm car and she could just be lulled into a false sense of security.

The Fox proved to be exactly as advertised. It smelled of leather and beeswax and old wood. Their room was huge; its four-poster was so big that a family could have slept in it. 'Good God!' said Alex blankly.

The landlord showed them how all the bathroom mechanics worked. He switched the bedside lights on and off in a helpful demonstration, offered them tea, supervised the boy who brought up their overnight bags and then closed the door on them.

Alex unpacked, trying to mask her unease. She had never shared a room with any man except Rupert. She was afraid it would show. So, she chatted brightly and kept the four-poster between them. She also did not meet his eyes.

Eventually, he said, 'Alex?'

'And then there's the clock in the marketplace...' She stopped. 'What?'

'Enough, already. I've had as much local detail as I can assimilate.'

'Oh.'

He came around the bed towards her, smiling. Alex whetted her lips and fixed her eyes on the bridge of his nose. That couldn't be too revealing, could it?

He said gently, 'You don't have to entertain me, you know.'

'But I...'

'You're jumpy as hell, and I don't blame you. You'll be better when this damned dance is over. In the meantime, let's not make it worse than it has to be, hmmm? Go run yourself a long bath. Soak. Relax.'

She swallowed. 'Thank you,' she said.

She sounded absurdly shy for a woman of her age and standing. She lifted her chin. 'That's a very good idea,' she said, trying to sound as if she discussed her bath-time arrangements with a man all the time. 'I even brought my favourite bath oil. I'll lob some in and indulge myself.'

'You deserve it. Just don't fall asleep in there.'

He did not touch her. But out of memory came the feeling of his hand against her cheek. Alex quivered with yearning.

'I...'

'I won't let you drown,' he promised, a smile in his voice.

The picture that he conjured up was too much for her. She grabbed her sponge bag and bolted for the bathroom.

'Relax,' she told herself, standing in front of a wall-to-ceiling mirror, breathing carefully. 'It will all be over in a few hours, and then you can get on with the rest of your life.'

She was not thinking about Laine's dance, either, though she had dreaded it for weeks.

Alex looked out into the bedroom, but Joe seemed to have gone for the moment. She whisked her dress into the bathroom before he got back and got dressed in there.

In a moment of defiance, she had opted for the topaz brocade she had bought herself, in spite of its bare shoulder and slashed skirt. Now she was undergoing a bad case of second thoughts. But she had no option – she had not brought another dress with her.

She came out of her room hesitantly.

Joe was back. He was unpacking his shoes, but he straightened when he heard the bathroom door.

'I was just going to launch a lifeboat...' He turned and stopped still, his eyes widening. 'When did you get *that*?'

'J-Julie said it was nice.' She was stammering a little.

What Julie had actually said, was that it was 'serious man-catcher gear'. But Alex was not about to tell Joe that.

Alex drew back. 'Is it too...?'

She looked at him in appeal.

He strolled forward.

'It is, indeed!' He took both her hands and held her away

from him, looking her up and down. 'Far too sexy to go out without an armed escort.' He sounded deeply amused.

Alex pulled her hands away.

It was one thing for Julie to say the dress was sexy in a dispassionate, female way in the cold light of day. It was quite another for Joe Gomez to stand in front of her, in the soft light of an evening bedroom, and say it in a voice that trickled down her shoulder blades like warm honey.

'I've made a mistake, haven't I?' she said. Not to him.

But he answered anyway, 'Depends on what you set out to do.'

'Well, I didn't set out to go to my half-sister's dance dressed in serious man-catcher gear,' she flashed back, unwisely.

His smile grew. 'I think you'll find your subconscious didn't agree with you.'

Alex was wringing her hands. 'I haven't got anything else to change into. What am I going to do?'

'See where it takes you,' he advised. He surveyed her, eyes narrowing. 'Jewellery?'

'I had thought of wearing my diamond-cluster earrings. Only, they're family heirlooms – and very rare because of the glint of gold in the diamonds – and I don't suppose my father's been able to give Laine anything comparable.' Alex knew she was babbling, but couldn't seem to stop. 'So… so it might give offence. What do you think…?' she added lamely.

Joe stuffed his hands in his pockets. His mouth took on a forbidding line.

'I think,' he said after a pause, 'that you ought to stop worrying about upsetting every damned neurotic you know – and just have a good time. If you like the diamonds, wear them.'

She gave him a tremulous smile. 'You're such a comfort, Joe. Thank you.'

He nodded, still grim. 'You're welcome.'

There was a note in his voice that Alex had not heard before.

'What is it?' she said uncertainly.

'Nothing.'

She searched his face. 'Tell me?'

He raised his eyebrows. 'You won't like it.'

Alex tilted her chin. 'I can take criticism. You've handed enough out these last few months.'

He shrugged. 'OK. It's not a good idea to tell a man he's a *comfort*. Kind of says you're not seeing him as a man. If you get my drift.'

Alex stared at him blankly. For a moment, she almost did not understand. And then...

The blush ran under her skin like a forest fire. She could feel it. She was incandescent with it. She pressed her hands to her cheeks.

'Told you,' said Joe, his eyes hard.

He waited for a moment, but Alex shook her head, speechless.

He went off to shower.

There was constraint between them as the powerful car snaked through the darkened lanes. Alex was conscious of the warmth of the body beside her, under its severe dinner jacket. But there was no meeting of minds. He felt as remote as the moon. When the black-clad arm brushed her bare shoulder, it was like being touched by an alien.

When they arrived, she stood awkwardly at the foot of the steps, not liking to take his arm. But Joe did not hesitate. He put an arm round her and swept her up the shallow steps into the party as if he had been doing it all his life. He lowered his head.

'You can do it, Alex,' he whispered in her ear.

Alex would have given anything for him to call her 'my love' just then, even though it was just a silly habit. Even though it meant nothing. But he didn't. It would have helped it he had said, 'You're beautiful,' or something like that. But he didn't do that, either.

So, she tilted her chin and marched into the party. She told herself she was lucky not to be going up those steps on her own. At least Joe was there. He had his arm round her for all to see.

You can't have everything, Alex reminded herself sternly. And with Joe as an escort, she had a lot more than she had ever expected. If she wanted even more… well, that was her problem.

She pinned on a smile and walked into the over-lit ballroom of the house that had once been her home yet was no longer, no matter what her father said.

Pretend home, she thought. *Pretend lover.*

Just then, her father broke away from a group of dinner-jacketed men and descended on them.

'Darling,' he said, too heartily.

Her father put his arm around her and held her against his shoulder rather convulsively. Alex tried hard not to notice that he was aiming this display of affection at a circulating photographer. She put one hand on his arm.

'Dad, this is Joe Gomez. You know I've gone into business with him.'

Her father lost some of his bonhomie.

'Gomez,' he said without enthusiasm. 'Good of you to give Alex a lift down.'

Joe gave him a glittering smile and took her back into the shelter of his own arm. It felt like steel round her ribs.

'I'm doing a lot more than that,' he told her father pleasantly. 'This is our first date. I'm going to spoil the life out of her.'

Oh, that word *spoil* again! Rubbing it in that she was only the latest in a procession of women to get the star treatment. Alex flinched, but kept her smile in place.

'Nice of you to ask us, Dad. The room looks great,' she added.

Joe looked down at her incredulously. The lovely linenfold panelling had been hung with purple-died mosquito netting, and adorned with various vaguely Arabic pictures and plaques.

Her father shifted uncomfortably. 'Yes, well. Laine and her mother decided that they wanted a harem theme,' he said uneasily. 'The young people are coming in fancy dress.'

Alex flinched silently, but Joe was more upfront. He laughed so loudly that people turned around to look.

'Well that puts us in our place,' he said, this time adding, 'My love.'

Alex leaned against him gratefully. Her father was flustered. 'I didn't mean... You never liked dressing up, even when you were a child, Alex. There was no intention to leave you out of anything.'

He looked so hot and bothered that she took pity on him.

'It's all right, Dad. You don't have to butter me up. I've already told Lavender that The Trust has to be fair to Laine.'

He hugged her, this time spontaneously. 'You're a sweetheart, Alex.'

'I agree,' said Joe suavely.

He detached Alex from her father with the possessiveness of a bodyguard. *Or a lover*, she thought, before she could stop herself.

'Enjoy yourselves,' said her father, accepting that possessive embrace at face value.

He was nervous of Joe, Alex could see. His bluff heartiness struck a false note as he added, 'There's a disco in the games room.'

Joe nodded and led Alex in the direction of the music. His hand felt hot against her side. She shivered deeply and pleasurably. He looked down at her, his expression enigmatic. But he said nothing.

The games room was nearly unrecognisable. It was lit like a smugglers' cavern, and was already full of gyrating bodies. Alex stopped dead.

'What on earth have they done to it?' she gasped. 'Where's the billiard table?'

'Over there under the bar, I guess,' said Joe, uninterested. 'Dance with me.' It was a command.

He swung her in front of him and began to move with his usual natural rhythm. Alex gulped and surrendered to the inevitable.

I can do this. Of course I can do this. I've always loved dancing. There's no reason why I shouldn't have a lot of fun dancing with Joe.

No reason at all, except that every time he touched her, her pulses leaped. And he touched her a lot.

Joe was not a man who believed in leaving his partner to do her own thing. He gave himself up to the music, and he made certain that Alex went with him every step of the way. By the time the disco stopped for a break, Alex was flushed and breathless. Joe was laughing. He ran a finger from her exposed nape to the indentation between her shoulder blades, to where the line of the brocade crossed her spine.

'Tantalising,' he said in her ear.

Alex could feel his breath stirring her hair. 'What is?'

'This dress. So near and yet so far.' He kneaded the back of her neck gently. 'Is that why you chose it?'

'What?' His stroking fingers were making it difficult to concentrate.

'I thought you'd wear that crimson dress. You looked so sensational in that.'

She had thought about it. She had even tried it on. But when she looked at herself in the mirror, she had remembered his intent eyes and that moment of total stillness while he looked at her. She told herself that the cleavage was too revealing. But it was not that, really. That dress was Joe's, somehow. She did not want to wear it for any old party, where he was with her, but not for the right reasons. She wanted him to want her. And if he did not, then the dress would stay unworn, which meant that it would probably languish in her wardrobe forever, Alex thought ruefully.

Aloud, she said, 'Oh, it didn't seem appropriate.'

He held her away from him, scanning her face. 'Why not? Oh, I suppose you're saving it for Sweetcroft.'

It was so far from the truth that Alex laughed aloud. But from the look he gave her, she could see that he thought she was agreeing with him.

He sighed. 'OK. I can take a hint. None of my business. Drink?'

'Oh, yes, of course. There should be some champagne, somewhere.'

She moved past him, out of the multi-coloured shadows into near-total darkness.

'There should indeed,' he murmured, dropping a kiss on her bare shoulder.

Alex nearly missed her step.

'In the dining room, I expect,' she said, sounding like a well-behaved child. When dazed, she always fell back on the good manners of childhood.

'Careful, my love. You're sounding like a kindergarten teacher again,' he murmured into her ear, so softly that no one else could possibly have heard. 'Just as well you don't dance like one.'

Joe laughed softly and moved his hand possessively round her waist. Alex swallowed hard.

'This way,' she said with determined brightness.

She should never have called him a comfort, Alex thought, her head whirling. That had to be the reason he was behaving like this. Even someone as relatively inexperienced as Alex could recognise that it was seriously provocative.

She contemplated telling him so. Then common sense reasserted itself.

Their path was blocked by a kissing couple. They were wrapped round each other, oblivious. The girl's scarlet-painted nails against the man's collar were the only things that were identifiable about them. But for some reason, some instinct, Alex was certain she knew those nails.

Her heart started to pound again. She reached for Joe's hand and held it hard.

'Alex!'

Joe was startled. Then warmly, terrifyingly, responsive. He caught her back against him, and she felt his body stir.

Oh no. It was anguish to pull away. Oh, why *now?*

But she did pull away. She had to.

'There's another way. Through the conservatory,' she muttered.

She could feel his confusion. She knew he was looking down at her in the darkness.

'Are you all right?'

'Yes. Yes, of course.'

But her hurried breathing must have told him she was not. He looked back over his shoulder at the lovers, still embracing.

The conservatory was the mansion's best claim to distinction. It had been planted more as indoor garden than a conservatory. It had narrow hedges of weeping fig and box, as well as a great climbing plumbago that scrambled twenty feet to the roof's arch. Tonight it was lit by flambeaux fixed in tubs among the greenery. And it was deserted.

Joe did not even pretend to look around.

'Very nice,' he said indifferently. 'What happened?'

'Nothing. I just felt a bit claustrophobic.'

For a moment he looked outrageously amused. 'Oh, is that what you call it?'

Alex could not help herself. She wanted to be in his arms

so badly. She laughed.

Joe smiled at her with such tenderness she hardly recognised him. 'That's better. Now tell me why you dragged me away from those two.'

Her laughter died. She said airily, 'I wanted you to see the conservatory.'

He chuckled. 'You're not much of a liar, Alex my love.'

The caressing note in his voice was almost her undoing. She could have cast herself into his arms and begged him to love her. For a moment, she almost did.

But it was too late. Dancing through the doors behind them came the girl they had just seen kissing wildly. Alex recognised the scarlet nails and harem slave-girl outfit. And they belonged to exactly who she thought they did. She could feel herself shrink and go cold.

Beside her, Joe stiffened. Alex looked up into his face, surprised. Did he already know Laine?

And then she looked back – and realised the identity of the man Laine had been kissing.

'Hello, Alex,' said Rupert uncomfortably.

Laine laced her scarlet-tipped hand through his arm and interlocked it with the fingers of her other hand. *He looks as if he's in a straitjacket*, thought Alex. She moved closer to Joe involuntarily.

'Alex,' said Laine, without pleasure. She did not offer to kiss her cheek. 'I didn't know you'd already got here.'

Rupert was absorbing Alex's changed appearance. His eyes lingered on her bare shoulder, the stylishly upswept hair. He looked taken aback.

'That's a very fetching dress,' he said with heavy gallantry.

Laine frowned. 'Have you seen Daddy?'

'Yes, we've had our photograph taken,' said Alex, trying not to feel bitter.

But Joe sensed it. The arm round her was rock steady. She leaned against him.

'Oh. Good.' Laine tightened her grip on Rupert's arm. 'Come on, darling. I want that ice cream. Then we can dance some more.'

She didn't even bother to say goodbye. Rupert looked over his shoulder grimacing humorously, but he allowed himself to be dragged away. Joe watched their departure in silence.

Alex was trembling uncontrollably.

'I see.' He said at last. 'Your sister, huh?'

'Yes.' She closed her lips over the word as if she would never speak again.

Joe drew a long breath. 'How long do we want to stay, Alex? No, scrub that. I know how long you want to stay: until everyone else has had their piece of you.' His voice was full of repressed rage – not very well-repressed rage. 'Have we satisfied them yet?'

She nodded. 'The photographs will get into the right magazines, so his business partners can see them. That's all Dad cares about, really.'

'Then let's go,' Joe said curtly.

There were deep grooves down his face. She had seen him look like that before. She stared at him, confused, not moving.

'Or do you want to stay? Maybe see if you can get Sweetcroft alone?' He flung it at her like a challenge.

'No,' she flung back.

They stood under the weeping figs, glaring at each other like duellists.

'Then let's go,' Joe said furiously.

Alex came to life. 'Yes. Yes, of course.'

People were finding the conservatory. Loud voices made the Victorian glass ring. Joe seized her hand and towed her through the gathering crowd. But on their way through the squash in the corridor, they came face to face with her father again.

'Alex! Not leaving so soon!' He looked alarmed. 'You

haven't fallen out with your stepmother? Or Laine? Please tell me you haven't.'

Joe stopped dead. He put Alex behind him and planted himself squarely in front of her father.

'Your daughter, Alex,' he said quietly, 'has been jumping through hoops to keep this family happy for as long as I have known her. It ends here.'

'What?' Her father tried to peer round him. 'Alex, what's this about?'

'Enough, already!' Joe demanded.

'Alex…'

Joe took a step towards him. He did not actually pick him up by the lapels, but it looked a close-run thing.

'You have a sweet, kind daughter who is too fair-minded for her own good. She is also too tender-hearted to tell you the truth. But I'm not. You're greedy, and you're a user.'

Her father gasped.

Joe's mouth was set in a harsh line. He looked like an avenging angel, thought Alex. She knew she ought to say something, but she seemed rooted to the spot.

'I'm here to tell you that you've used Alex for the last time,' he said flatly. 'From here on in, you sort out your money problems on your own. That goes for your fights with your appalling mother, too. Alex won't be broking any more peace settlements with Lavender. And she won't be picking up any more bills for that grabbing little piece who has just stolen her boyfriend.'

Her father went puce.

'My own father was a shifty bastard,' said Joe with an intensity that made her father take a step backwards. 'But by God, he never did to me what you've done to Alex. Now, get out of my way.'

He reached behind him, not looking to see whether she was there or not. He knew.

Alex put her hand in his.

'Alex, you can't walk out like this.' Her father's voice rose to a wail. 'What will people *say?*'

She pulled at Joe's hand. They stopped. He turned black, narrowed eyes on her.

She thought: *this is critical.*

She said sadly, 'I'm sorry, Dad. Joe's right.'

'*Alex*!'

'I'm sorry you and Mother broke up. I'm sorry for everything. But it's not my fight. I'm not getting involved again.'

Joe was very still.

'Ever,' she said steadily. 'Joe's right. Take me out of here, Joe.'

chapter twelve

Alex did not speak in the car. She was still shaking with reaction. In the whole wretched family fight, she had repressed her real feelings for so long that she had almost forgotten she had any. When Joe had blasted her father like that, she had suddenly felt she didn't have to try any more. She felt free.

But along with the freedom came a terrible uncertainty.

Joe only spoke once. 'You all right?'

Alex bit her lip. She did not trust herself to speak, though she could feel his quick, sideways glance of concern. In the end she nodded.

'*Bastard!*' Joe slammed his hand against the steering wheel as if it was a personal enemy. The great car shot forward and was curbed.

He did not speak again. And when they pulled into the courtyard of the old coaching inn, he helped her into the silent building as if she were weak with illness.

What an idiot he must think me. Can't stand up to my father for years. And when I do, I go into freefall, Alex thought. But still she leaned against him gratefully.

A fire had been lit in their room. Joe strode forward and threw another couple of logs on it. As the sparks burst up, he pulled her into the old leather chair beside the fire and took one of her hands. It was icy.

He looked down, startled, and began to chafe it between both of his hands.

'It's not the end of the world, Alex. Everyone rows. Do things they regret.' His voice shook with suppressed fury suddenly, 'Some people even take the hint and cut their losses.'

Alex stared at him, silent.

Joe sighed. Then his tone gentled. 'Nobody gets through a relationship without the odd spat, my love. But don't you think this thing with Rupert has gone far enough?'

She shook her head, momentarily bewildered.

'Look. I don't know what he was like when you were a child, but he's shit now. He dumped you, screwed your sister, and left you to find out in the middle of everyone.'

She opened her mouth to protest, but stopped.

Joe raised his hand. 'And don't tell me we don't know he's screwing your sister, because you saw them too. They weren't trying to hide it.'

Alex found her voice then. 'I...I already knew.'

'It was coming off them in waves...' Joe broke off. His voice sharpened. 'What do you mean, you already knew?'

And somehow it was the worst thing of the whole evening. All the betrayal, all the sheer unkind contempt of Rupert's behaviour, rose up like a monster to leer at her. Joe was looking at her as if he was not *surprised.* As if she was the sort of woman who just asked to be cheated on.

She shut her eyes. 'I tried to phone him in New York. I called his hotel room.' She opened her eyes. 'A girl answered. They were in bed. My call woke her up.' Alex began to laugh. 'It's classic, really.'

She flung her head back. Her whole body shook with uncontrollable laugher. It spiralled up the scale, out of control. Alex could hear herself, but was powerless to stop.

Joe slapped her face.

Alex's laughter died as if he had thrown water on a fire. She stared at him, one hand to her smarting cheek.

'You hit me!' she said disbelievingly.

The heavy eyebrows were locked in an intimidating frown. His face looked thin and angry, all cheekbones and little violent flickers of light in the impenetrable eyes.

'I can't stand hysterical women,' Joe said curtly. 'Tell me what happened. No shrieking, please,' he added in warning.

Alex swallowed. Now that the banshee's laughter had died out of her, she felt cold. She was also beginning to realise that she felt shocked and sick, as if she'd been run over by one of the demolition machines Joe's clients used on their big building sites.

She gave him a concise account of what she had heard. She spoke in a cool, controlled little voice.

'Oh God,' he said when she'd finished. He was still holding her hands. He squeezed them. 'You really didn't have any idea up until then?'

She answered quietly, desolation rising in her voice, 'No.'

He muttered something violently under his breath.

All her defences, all the decent reticence of ordinary living, seemed to have been blasted away in the shock. She was hardly aware that it was Joe she was talking to, and that he might not want to hear the intimate details of her life. She was thinking aloud, painfully.

'I think I must be very stupid about…oh, men and sex and everything. I mean, I know the rules. I'm not a fool, and it's not exactly hard to learn. I used to watch my school friends when they first started to date. I could see how it was done, what you were supposed to feel, to say. But – I never wanted to.'

Joe made a protesting movement, quickly stilled.

'Rupert was always terribly dashing, terribly popular. I knew he was out of my league. But he had been so *kind* when I was a child. I thought there was a bond. When we both came to London and he seemed to take an interest in me at last, I could hardly believe it.'

'Take an interest,' said Joe between his teeth. 'Like *The Prince and the Beggar Maid*? What bloody nonsense did he sell you, Alex?'

She smiled faintly. 'Oh, it isn't nonsense. He's quite a catch, is Rupert. And I'm not. I never have been. I'm not even any good at sex. I can't seem to get the hang of it somehow.

Can't…what was it you said?… *abandon* myself. Yes, that's it. I can't abandon myself.'

Joe snorted.

She said dreamily, 'It's some sort of magic. But I don't understand it. Rupert has it. You have it. Julie has it. Charlie and the boy genius have it. I haven't. I'm not really…well, I suppose the word is *marriageable*.'

Joe said something extremely rude. It startled Alex out of her gentle remoteness. Joe hardly ever swore. Or looked fierce enough to kill. Momentarily, she quailed.

He said in a voice of extreme self-control, 'What on earth do you think you're talking about?'

Alex was surprised. 'Marriage.'

'Oh,' said Joe with heavy irony. 'I'm glad to have that cleared up. You're sure you don't mean some secret society?'

'Nothing secret about it,' said Alex sadly. 'It's there for all to see. What everyone does. Except me. Maybe I'm too much like my mother. Lots of talents, just none of them for marriage.'

Joe's expression became singularly inscrutable. He said crisply, 'Anyone who married you would be extremely lucky.'

Alex nodded. 'Yes, I think so too.'

Joe became slightly less inscrutable. His brows flew up. She smiled, glad to have disconcerted him for once.

'I'd be a good bargain,' she went on in her most reasonable tones. 'I'm faithful and house-trained, and I don't make scenes.'

Joe uttered a strangled noise. 'Faithful and house-trained? Is that what Sweetcroft told you?'

'He didn't have to tell me. I could see it for myself.'

'Perceptive of you.'

'I am perceptive,' Alex agreed serenely. 'And competent. Liberated. I can look after myself. No husband would have to worry himself sick about having to look after me.' She laughed a little, but it sounded off-key. 'I can even pay my own bills.'

Joe's eyebrows met over his nose in a fearsome frown. Not a vestige of inscrutability remained. He looked furious.

'A paragon,' he snapped.

Alex considered that for a moment. Then shook her head.

'No,' she said fairly. 'Not a paragon. Not a bad bargain, but not a paragon.' She drew a deep breath. 'I suppose that's what I thought Rupert had decided.'

Joe made a disbelieving noise.

She tried to explain. 'I suppose I always knew that Rupert's head was ruling his heart when he decided to marry me. He could see the advantages.' She swallowed first, then added with all the lightness she could muster, 'Not because he couldn't help himself.'

If she thought Joe would sympathise, she was disappointed.

Joe said coldly, 'Horse feathers.'

Alex jumped. 'What?'

'Your theory, as I understand it, is that you are not the sort of woman men fall in love with. This is because you lack some sort of magical aura.'

'I didn't say "magic"…'

He took no notice. 'And that Rupert Sweetcroft, of all people, is walking proof that this total lack of self-worth is justified.'

Alex said dryly, 'Rupert isn't the only man in the world who doesn't want me.'

'Stop right there,' said Joe. It was not much above a whisper. He sounded angry.

She blinked, suddenly taking in his expression. It was not just angry. It was *dangerous*.

'What does that make me?' he said between his teeth.

'What?'

'No man wants you? What the hell do you think I am?'

'I…'

'You know I want you. I've told you in every way I can. I've shown you. Hell…you knew what was happening to me on that bloody dance floor this evening.'

Alex had a vivid recollection of stepping back against him when they first saw Laine and Rupert twined round each other. How Joe had felt. How she had responded. And how, for a moment, she had not given a damn for the kissing couple, or anyone but themselves. How she had wanted him for weeks now.

She flushed painfully. 'You'd be disappointed,' she muttered.

'Excuse me?'

'I told you.' Her voice was almost inaudible. 'I'm *terrible* at sex.'

Joe flung his hands up in a gesture of exasperation. 'You…'

He gave up and hauled her out of the chair into his arms. Alex put out a startled hand to save herself. It was no good. He crushed her to him.

His jacket was open. She could feel the warm, slow beat of his heart under her fingers. He looked as if he was on the rack.

'What is it?' she said, alarmed. 'Joe?'

'Oh, what's the use?' His hands were hard on her upper arms. He was hurting her.

Alex tilted her head all the way back to look up at his face, and saw that he had no idea of it. And then he moved, grappling her to him clumsily. Joe, who was never clumsy! He looked positively satanic.

And amazingly attractive.

She felt her body jerk. The slow, insistent pulse she had heard before began to throb through her. *Help*, she thought. *Here I go lusting after Joe Gomez again. And he's much too close not to know this time.*

He knew.

It was a harsh, expert kiss, and Alex went up in flames. When he'd kissed her that night in Lavender's darkened office, he had set light to a fire, thought Alex muzzily. It had been smouldering ever since, even when she had turned him down. Perhaps most when she turned him down. It did not have one single thing to do with Rupert Sweetcroft, his betrayal or the whole cold war that was her family life. It had nothing to do with anything except Joe and how she felt for him.

How she felt about him. Alex went cold with shock, then hot as fire as she realised what that meant. The alien arms around her were hard, as if they were not made of muscle and bone at all, but some violent magnetic mineral. It was frightening. But not half as frightening as the way she could feel an answering force in herself. Not for the first time, she acknowledged.

Oh yes, he knew.

She heard him say, 'I should have done this long ago.'

The ancient floorboards creaked in the silent room as he carried her to the bed. They made her jump. Joe gave a soft, excited laugh and held her to his chest possessively.

'You're sure? Sure you want this?'

She did, of course she did. But shyness was a padlock. She could not say it.

Instead, she dropped her head on his shoulder. It was a sign of total acceptance, and they both knew it.

As he lowered her among the pillows, her hands were already tugging at his shirt, his unfamiliar bow tie. He did not ask her any more questions that she could not answer. And he was a good deal more efficient with the fastenings on her clothes than she was with his.

Alex – tidy, efficient Alex – did not notice where he tossed her dress. Or anything else, for that matter. There was no more room for doubt. Her throbbing body would not permit any more excuses.

As his hand swept masterfully down her body, she seemed to come alive. More than alive… she became *beautiful*. It was as if his touch could turn her dull flesh to living gold.

Magic.

The flaming logs sent wild shadows round the room. He looked like a vision of fire, the fantasy pursuer from her dreams.

But when she touched him, he was not fire or fantasy. He was hard, demanding flesh. And she could make him shake convulsively. She wanted to.

I'm abandoning myself at last, Alex thought, amazed.

She had never imagined this; never dreamed that this was what she wanted; never dreamed that this was what she could do to a man she loved.

But now she knew. And she was helpless to control it. She was riding an elemental wave that had come from nowhere. If she died of it, she could not stop. And nor could he.

Joe gasped. 'Oh God, Alex. *Alex...!*' And the last vestiges of control slipped from her clenching hands, unregretted.

When Alex woke up, she found she was alone. The fire was out, and the sheet was on the floor. But that didn't matter. What did matter was that Joe had gone – and she was all alone.

'What went wrong?' said Joe, exasperated.

They were driving back to London, as Alex had insisted. The road was bleak and windswept, and nearly empty. She had not even wanted to stop for breakfast.

Breakfast had been the second thing to go wrong.

First, there was waking up alone. The sense of abandonment was a killer.

By the time Joe got back, she was out of bed and trying to poke the fire back into life with inexpert violence. He was fully dressed, she saw. The terrible inner chill went deeper.

Joe did not notice.

'Let me do that,' he said. 'You'll never get it started that way. You're losing all the heat.'

He brushed her aside, smiling.

Smiling and relaxed, and so damned sexy that she could have flung herself into his arms right then, if it wasn't for the chill of being left alone. If it wasn't for feeling unloved.

Alex folded her arms around herself, shivering in spite of the terry-towelling robe she was wearing.

Joe piled the ashy logs together in the middle of the grate and went down on his knees, applying old-fashioned bellows to flame the fire.

Over his shoulder he said, 'Get back into bed and keep warm. The central heating in this place is strictly for background support.'

Alex dived back into the four-poster. She did not take off the hotel's complimentary bathrobe before she pulled the covers up to her chin.

Joe blew the fire into some very satisfactory flames before coming over to her. He raised his eyebrows quizzically. 'You *were* cold, weren't you? Never mind, I'm here now. Move over.'

'No,' shouted Alex.

He stopped.

'What?' he asked blankly.

The chill was like a knife turning and turning in her heart. She hurt so much that she wanted to hurt back. She said the nastiest thing she could think of. 'Even Rupert,' she told him in a hard voice, 'managed to stay until I woke up.'

After that, things went from bad to worse. She did not know where the accusations came from. She had never behaved like that in her life before. She flung stuff at him that she had not even known she minded about.

The flirtations. The bets on the staying power of his previous girlfriends. The careful avoidance of commitment. Even their own undignified tussle on the office floor when she nearly went mad with lust.

At first, Joe tried to argue. Then he went silent. A little muscle worked in his jaw.

Eventually, he said, 'Where the hell did I get the idea that you were a reasonable woman?'

And then he slammed out.

Maybe they might have patched it up at breakfast. Alex felt more like her old self once she had showered and dressed. She was still hurt, but a lifetime effort of always seeing the other person's point of view had reasserted itself. And Joe had been out for a walk and come back with icy dew in his hair and a determined air of calm.

So they might have made it back to some sort of truce. But then she saw what he had ordered for her breakfast.

Marmalade sandwiches. *Marmalade sandwiches!* Straight off that wicked seducer's wish list he had made her give him all those weeks ago.

'Nice to see the old technique doesn't desert you in moments of crisis,' said Alex affably, hating him.

Joe was bewildered. 'What technique?'

Alex flicked a finger at the nursery food. 'Spoiling me, right?'

For the first time since he had built up the fire in their bedroom, he smiled. 'What's wrong with that?'

'What's wrong,' said Alex between her teeth, 'is that it's calculated.'

'So are half the best things in life.'

She could have hit him.

'Like last night, I suppose?'

He stopped smiling. 'What do you mean?'

'Julie always said you had to be a red-hot lover. I must remember to tell her she was right,' she told the window airily.

For a moment she thought she had gone too far. He threw the napkin away from him and stood up. 'Come on. We're leaving. *Now.*'

He drove the big Jensen Healey with the precision of a man

at the end of his tether. They were on the outskirts of London before he opened his lips again.

'I don't understand what happened.'

Alex was looking firmly out of the window. They were passing a street market. The cheerfully jostling Christmas crowds recalled her first dream, and she shuddered.

'Last night was a mistake.'

His hands tightened on the wheel. 'Oh yeah? Well, don't give me that "I-don't-like-sex" crap, because I don't believe it. You liked it, all right.'

Alex could not deny it. She shrugged, still not looking at him. 'So what? So I liked the sex. You liked the sex. And that was last night.'

There was a pause. 'You make it sound ugly,' Joe said slowly.

'Do I? How odd. I thought that was exactly what you were suggesting in Venice.'

'Don't twist it. You know what I wanted in Venice.'

She gave a harsh laugh. 'And last night you got it. Game over.'

'Look, Alex, what's this about? Are you saying you *didn't* want to make love last night?'

'Love!' She poured all the scorn into it she could manage.

A truck pulled out in front of them, and he had to brake. For a few minutes, he concentrated on the traffic. When they had got through the worst, he said in a calmer voice, 'I thought love was involved.'

Alex clenched her teeth so hard against the pain that she could hear her ears ring.

She said coolly, 'I think I must have had a small crush on you. Not surprising, I suppose.'

'*What?*' Joe sounded genuinely shocked.

'Don't worry. I've never had a crush before. But from what I've read, you get over it quite quickly.'

'You do indeed,' he said savagely.

He did not say another word until he drew the big car to a halt outside the mews house. He turned off the ignition and sat there for a moment, not speaking.

Alex started to unbuckle her seat belt. He stopped her.

'Look, Alex,' he said quietly. 'Tell me the truth.'

'I've told you…'

'No. I'm not buying the "schoolgirl crush" line. You're no schoolgirl. And I sure as hell am no heartthrob.'

'Want to bet on it?' she muttered.

He ignored that. 'This is about that garbage pail you handed me in Venice, isn't it? "I'm a one-man woman." So, don't ask me to open my closed little mind and look at what's actually going on…?'

Alex bounced around in her seat. It was a struggle against the seatbelt, but she ignored the constriction as she glared at him.

'I *was* a one-man woman.'

'No, you weren't,' Joe countered.

She flinched, remembering her own weak-kneed fantasies about this very man, now sitting here looking at her with hard eyes. Oh yes, Rupert had betrayed her. But hadn't she betrayed him first, with her response to Joe Gomez and his box of sexy tricks?

Hating herself as much as him, she said intensely, 'Well, I should have been.'

'No, you shouldn't. Hasn't done your mother much good, has it?'

She gasped. 'That was a low blow.'

'No it wasn't. It was the truth.' He sounded almost frantic. 'Alex, look, I don't know if you've been trying to re-run your parents' lives or what, but that thing you had for Sweetcroft – it was crazy.'

Alex was incandescent with rage. She sprung the seatbelt and jumped out of the car.

Joe followed more slowly. He leaned on the hood, not taking his eyes off her.

'Nobody falls in love when they're six and stays that way. No matter how loyal they are. It's just not realistic.'

'You don't know a thing about it…'

'You didn't fall in love,' he said steadily. 'You settled for the safe option. You took a decision, and called it "love".'

Alex gasped with rage. 'Oh, I see. You think I was afraid of being left on the shelf.'

'That's not what I said.'

She ignored his protest, but she was so angry she could barely get the words out.

'I was afraid of being lonely. So I "*settled for*…" That's what you said, wasn't it? So I "settled for" Rupert…?'

'Oh no,' said Joe heavily. 'I think you had the full McCoy for Rupert. I think you'd talked yourself into it. And I think you're not going to give anyone else a chance, out of sheer pig-headedness. All because of a delusion.'

So there was a third reason to hate him.

Alex was speechless. She slammed into the house without even trying to find the words to tell him what she thought of him.

Behind her, Joe yelled, 'And I think it's a wicked waste!'

He brought her case round later. Alex refused to go to the door, so Julie took the delivery and returned, subdued.

'He looks terrible. Won't you at least talk to him?'

'Never.'

'That's going to be difficult. Or are you going to walk out of the job as well?'

Alex hadn't thought of that. 'I suppose I'll have to.'

She was not surprised at how bleak it made her feel. Hating Joe, she found, did not stop her going weak at the knees whenever she thought of him. If only he hadn't left her alone this morning. If only his technique wasn't so well honed. If only he hadn't spoiled so many other girl friends – or not tried to spoil Alex.

If only he loved her.

She grabbed the bag he had delivered and laundered its contents ruthlessly.

Nevertheless, she managed to get herself together enough to go to work on Monday morning. She was early, but Joe was earlier. He was heavy-eyed and unshaven, but his manner was impeccable. She would never have believed he could sound so unemotional.

Professional at last, thought Alex. It broke her heart.

The only time he showed some of the hidden fire was when she suggested tentatively that she leave.

His eyes flashed. 'No.'

'But…'

'I said *no!*'

'But it can't do your work any good to have me around, reminding you of our… differences.'

His eyes narrowed to diamond-hard slits.

'You pushed for this partnership,' he said grimly. 'You'll bloody well stick with it.'

Alex's sense of fair play had been restored by the worst night of her life. So she could only concede that he was in the right.

'If that's what you want,' she said unhappily.

He said something unprintable and banged out.

Still, they got through somehow. The office party was bad. Joe danced with Fran like a wild man, and all the younger architects' girlfriends drooled over him. Alex developed a genuine headache and went home early.

Everyone talking about their Christmas plans was bad, too. Alex did not mind spending Christmas alone. Heaven knows, she had done it before, and enjoyed it. But somehow, with Joe talking about going to Tom Skelton's jolly family for Christmas Day, this time she felt inexplicably rejected.

In the end, she and Julie went to a Christmas-morning service at church and ended up doing a round of mince pie-and-mulled wine parties in the mews, which felt positively Dickensian. They were stimulating and heart-warming, but they didn't dispel the feeling of rejection.

I want Joe, Alex admitted to herself.

And then she admitted something else: *I never wanted Rupert like this.*

It frightened her.

After Christmas, work was better. Now that enough distributors had signed, Alex had agreed that filming could start in Venice. Tom went there immediately after the New Year.

Joe followed two days later. He took Fran with him to search for some of the venues her research had uncovered. Alex did her best not to feel jealous, but it didn't work.

She had never been really jealous before, either. That was even more frightening. She was exceptionally nice to Fran when the girl got back, and Joe went on to discuss a commission in Hamburg.

He kept on the move for the whole of January. Some of his itinerary was already in the diary. Quite a lot of it was new. Alex knew he was giving her room to simmer down, and tried hard to be grateful.

Meanwhile, they communicated by email. Politely.

Eventually, they graduated to talking on the telephone. Joe told her stories about pompous aldermen that made her laugh. Once or twice, they even managed to be quite friendly.

January turned into February. Alex's snowdrops emerged in the white-painted tub outside her front door.

And then Joe lobbed the bombshell.

It was waiting for her on the email when she got in to work: clear, detailed instructions, down to the books she was to bring and the clothes she was to pack. Tickets were arranged.

Why? wondered Alex. Booking flights was her job or Fran's. Joe never did it. So why had he taken on that chore now?

But of course, the answer was obvious: because he knew that if he didn't, she would have a found a way of getting out of it.

She had known they would have to come face to face, once again. She had braced herself for it every day for weeks. But not like this. Not with Robert Browning's *Collected Poems* and the ruby-velvet dress in her luggage.

Not in *Venice*.

chapter thirteen

Alex was packing when Julie scratched on her door.

'Your mum's on the phone. She wants to come round.'

'When?' said Alex, hunting distractedly for tights.

'Now.'

Alex's heart sank. Sounded like a crisis. 'She can't. I'm on my way to Venice this afternoon. I haven't got time for this.'

Julie made a face, still hovering.

'All right. I suppose you can't tell her that. I'll come,' Alex said.

She picked up the telephone and said crisply, 'I don't work for Lavender any more, Mother. If you've got a problem, ask Gerald.'

'No problem.' Caroline sounded as if she was laughing. 'But I do need to see you.'

Alex looked at her watch. 'You can come with me to the airport, if you like. But I've got to leave in the next hour.'

Caroline arrived in Lavender's limousine. If Alex had not been hovering in the sitting room while she was waiting, she would not have recognised her. Her mother was wearing a smart red coat and a black Cossack hat. Her knee-length boots shone. And her eyes were dancing.

'Wow, Mrs Eyre, you look like a million dollars,' said Julie, opening the door.

She and Alex exchanged wild eyebrow semaphores, and then Alex stowed her suitcase and dived into the car.

'See you, Julie. I'll let you know when I'm coming back.'

Julie grinned and closed the passenger door on her. 'Give my regards to The Red-Hot Lover.'

'Oh sure,' said Alex. 'In those words, if you like.'

Julie stepped back and waved as the car pulled out. Alex braced herself for her interrogation. But her mother had another priority today.

'Darling, I wanted you to be the first to know,' she said, trying unsuccessfully to stop beaming. 'Gerald and I are getting married.'

Alex's draw dropped. 'Gerald? Our Gerald? Eyre Associates' Managing Director Gerald?'

Caroline nodded like an excited schoolgirl.

Alex gave up. 'When did this happen?'

'Well, he took me away for Christmas. He said he thought I needed a rest. Well, I was doing that job so badly. Honestly, darling, I have no idea how you kept so many balls in the air. Anyway, Lavender was being bloody and she made me cry, and Gerald said, "What about Mallorca?". And there we were.'

Caroline spread her hands in a magician's revelatory gesture. Her nails were painted the same colour as her coat.

Was this the same woman whom Alex had had to prise out of her apartment with threats only four months ago? She could hardly believe it. But those scarlet nails convinced her. She beamed, hugging her mother.

'Congratulations.'

'I'm so happy.

'I can see you are. Love is a wonderful thing,' Alex said devoutly.

'Yes.' Caroline sighed beatifically. She purred for a moment, then changed the subject. 'Now tell me about you. Who's this red-hot lover?'

'A stupid joke. I'm going to Venice to work.'

Caroline was disappointed, but not surprised. *And who whould blame her*, thought Alex with irony.

She said, 'Darling, I know you've given Rupert his marching orders. And I wanted you to know, I'm really glad.'

'Are you?' Alex was fascinated. 'But I thought you…'

'I was stupid. As if any man at all was better than no man. I don't know why I wasted all those years mooning over your father. I know that now.'

'Good for Gerald.'

Caroline gave a naughty giggle. 'Yes. Um… Alex…' Caroline looked uneasily at the chauffeur and lowered her voice. 'I'm sort of worried I may have encouraged you to do the same thing.'

'You didn't encourage me to do anything, Mother. My mistakes were all my own work,' said Alex gently.

'You were always such a kind little girl,' said Caroline, her eyes filling. 'Listen, darling, I've been a rotten mother, but I have learned this. You've got to trust your instincts about people.'

'What?'

'If you hadn't unloaded Rupert already, I'd be here telling you to get rid of him at once. Oh, I know I was always telling you to be sensible. Think about consequences. Plan. I bet your father said the same. But you can't plan things like falling in love,' Caroline said earnestly. 'When it happens, you just have to go with the flow. And if it doesn't happen, then you just have to get on with your life until it does.'

Alex looked at her mother. She was transformed. She knew she was loved, and she was glowing with it. It was impressive.

She nodded slowly. 'I'll remember that.'

She continued mulling it over during the flight, on her arrival at the hotel and after the enthusiastic greeting she got from Tom and his assistant. In fact, she only listened to their account of the first couple of days' shooting with half an ear.

It was when Tom said, 'Joe said he needed you,' that she tuned in properly.

'Why does he need me? I got all the permissions to film sorted out before Christmas.'

'Yes, but he says he needs you to tell it to.'

Alex stared. 'What?'

'It's true, too,' admitted Tom. 'He knows his stuff, but he's no good unless he's got an audience. He needs to see a reaction. I'm stuck behind a camera, and Rick is messing about with sound. So Joe ends up sounding like he's reading off an autocue. He's no good without you.'

'How true,' said a deep voice behind them.

They all turned. It was Joe. He was smiling at Alex as if he had never seen anything so lovely.

She almost looked over her shoulder to see who was getting that high-voltage appreciation. But she knew it was for her, really; her instinct told her.

The last thing Caroline had said, waving her off into the departure queue, had been, 'Listen to your heart, Alex. When it comes to love, instincts are better than logic.'

Thank you, mother.

She said slowly, 'Hello, Joe.'

Something lit in his eyes.

'I'm glad you came, Alex.'

It sounded as if he had not been entirely sure that she would, in spite of all his efficient arrangements.

She nodded. 'So am I.'

His eyes bored into hers. There was a question in their depths. But they were not alone, and Tom wanted to discuss the next day's work. Anyway, Alex did not know the answer. She only knew that she had questions too – and that her instincts told her they would need to be resolved very soon.

Tom and his assistant seemed as if they never went to bed. Alex tried to outstay them, but she soon realised there was no hope of that. She stayed in the bar discussing the next day's filming as long as she could, but her eyelids were drooping. Eventually, she yawned openly.

Joe took a decision. 'Time you were in bed,' he said, standing up. 'I'll walk you to the elevator.'

The hotel could not have been more different from the old coaching inn. It was full of chandeliers and purpose-woven carpet, with rococo wall mouldings and enormous gilded urns of golden grasses in every alcove. And everywhere there were masks.

'Sinister,' said Alex, shivering a little at the sight of one chequerboard mask with a great spur of a nose and violently dyed feathers in a crest above it. 'Those empty eyes.'

'Ah, but the eyes belong to the wearer,' said Joe. 'It's not empty. The mask is a keeper of secrets. The wearer watches, and all you can see is his painted smile.'

Alex shivered again. Joe did not press the ornate button that summoned the lift. Instead, he leaned one arm against the wall and looked down at Alex. 'Like your English upper-class manners, wouldn't you say?' he drawled.

She sighed. 'Don't start that again, Joe. Class is outdated. And if I hide my feelings, that's because it's what I do. Not because I think it's a good thing. In fact, I'm not sure it *is* such a good thing.'

His eyes gleamed. 'That sounds interesting.'

She gave an enormous yawn. 'But I'm not up to discussing it tonight.'

He laughed and let her off. 'I can see that. All right. Good night, my love.'

'Ah.' She stopped yawning long enough to make a decision to trust her instincts. 'Joe…'

'Here.'

'Don't call me that,' Alex said quietly.

The gleam died out of his eyes as if someone had thrown a bucket of soot on the flames. 'Not "my love"?'

Alex hesitated. But she was too tired to weigh her words, and her mother had said instincts were better than logic.

'Not unless you mean it.'

Joe's jaw dropped. And then the lift arrived.

He took a passionate step forward. But it was too late. Alex was already in the lift, headed for her room and too-long-delayed sleep.

'Damn,' he said, smacking the wall in frustration.

But when he went back to the others, he was wearing a deep, private smile.

The next day, Alex found that she had to be the presence just out of sight, to whom Joe told the story of Venice. 'My mystery lady,' he said in a caressing voice.

Alex blushed. But both Tom and the assistant took it in their stride.

They were standing on the quayside of one of the narrow waterways. It was cold in the early morning shadow, although out on the Grand Canal the water was turning gold in the sunrise. Mist curled up from the gondoliers' poles. The mediaeval brickwork of Renaissance palaces shone with unearthly light.

Tom was enchanted. He could hardly stop imagining pictures of the magical place.

'We'll get you a mask and you can be behind the credits, Alex,' he promised, between pointing and balancing, and framing shots with his hands. 'You'll need one for Carnival, anyway.'

'Carnival? Surely that's not yet?'

'In theory, it runs from Saint Stephen's Day to Shrove Tuesday,' Joe told her. 'But the big party starts ten days or so before Lent begins.'

Alex calculated. 'But that's now.'

'The opening ball is tonight,' Joe said smugly.

'We've even got permission to take the camera in,' Tom's assistant added.

Alex began to understand why Joe had told her to bring the ruby dress. She met his eyes, and nothing in the world could have prevented her from shivering at what she saw there. It was a promise, uncomplicated and blatant. Something deep inside her began to stir and stretch. Her shivering had nothing to do with the February chill in the air.

'Goodness knows why we need permission, since the whole point of a mask is to hide your identity.'

'I thought it was to hide your feelings,' murmured Alex.

Joe's eyes were like a caress on her skin. 'That, too. Gamblers were supposed to wear one to make sure their expressions did not give them away. Venice has always had a very bad name for gamblers.'

She pursed her lips and saw him watch her mouth as if it fascinated him.

Help, she thought. *This can't go on. I'm going to jump on him with the camera running if he keeps looking at me like that*.

Logic told her to cool it. Instinct said… instinct said 'go for it'.

So, she lowered her lashes and said softly, 'And are you a gambler, Joe?'

'I never thought so. Maybe I should try it.'

It was like wearing masks, having this private conversation while all around them Venetians piled into *vaporetti* to go to work, and Tom and his assistant plotted shots. It was exciting and dangerous, and yet utterly secret.

'Who needs a mask?' said Alex under her breath.

And Joe, the polished flirt and practised spoiler of women, groaned as if he were in real pain.

It was like that all day. Everything he said – everything Alex did in response – carried a private meaning.

'Venice,' said Joe to the camera, looking at Alex, 'is an enigma. Always was. Half counting-house, half mirage.'

'I can't afford to lose myself in a mirage,' she'd said to him, the last time they were here. Now he was challenging her to say it again.

He saw that she understood and smiled, the gypsy face alive with amused satisfaction.

'Great,' Tom said from behind his camera with enthusiasm.

'God, the camera loves, you jammy beggar.'

'And what a mirage,' Joe continued to the camera. 'If Venice was married to the sea, her lovers were the rest of the world. Greece and Rome. Byzantium and Antioch. Arabia Felix, where she found the spice traders. Cathay, where she found a culture as strange as science fiction is to us. And all of those ideas were brought back here to build – in this delta where no one in his right mind would build a hen coop – this queen of cities.'

He led them through the alleyways. He talked well. He knew his stuff, and was fascinated by the interplay of East and West, utilitarian and sheer, exuberant extravagance. But the real charm was his love for the stones.

Alex watched him stroke the weathered stone façade of the Palazzo Grimani, and shivered as if it was her flesh he was touching.

'And so much of Venice is deceptive,' he told her. 'Look at this great Palace. It was built in 1556. We had only known of America for just over fifty years. Nearly every building in London or Paris was made of wood. But here we have brick and stone. And not just brick and stone – but brick and stone that plays games with us. Teases us.'

His mouth tilted as Alex blushed.

'Look at it from the Grand Canal, and you see a massive structure, almost a temple or a cathedral. Three huge floors. Great arched galleries overlooking the water. How it must have dwarfed the people who lived here, we think. And how grand they must have thought they were to commission such a thing.'

'But look down the side of the building. The Venetians were practical people. They worked here as well as living and strutting and showing off. They knew floor space had a price, and Venetians have never been wasteful. In reality, each one of those huge vaulted floors was divided into two.'

Alex looked. She saw he was right.

'Amazing,' she said, forgetting she was not supposed to speak. Tom would have to edit it out of the tape, and she knew that was a nuisance. But she had not been able to stop herself.

Joe sent her a look that was more of a kiss than many of Rupert's conscientious farewell embraces.

'Always take your time to look at Venice,' said the voice of honeyed seduction five feet away. 'Your eyes won't deceive you as long as you pay attention.'

Alex decided it would be just as well not to meet his eyes for the rest of the day – not if it continued to have this effect on her pulses.

They hired a gondola for the whole day, and took it slowly along the Grand Canal. Sometimes the water was so black, it almost looked like tarmac. Then as the lights came on, it began to turn into the place of mystery that Alex had seen before. For every palazzo, there was its glimmering reflection, moving and dancing in the rippling water. It was as if there was another city that just could not keep still, only half a heartbeat out of reach.

'Nothing is what it seems in Venice,' said Joe.

Alex looked up. It had got quite dark. The mists of the day had rolled away, and the sky was frosted with stars. Outside, one of the palazzi people were lighting great flambeaux.

'What a night,' she sighed softly.

They were sitting at the opposite end of the boat from the gondolier's lantern. Tom was poring over his schedule with a pocket torch held by his assistant. Unseen, Joe took her hand.

'There's never been a night like this,' he said. For the first time in the whole day, he sounded serious.

Alex felt her mouth go dry. She turned her hand in his, returning the pressure of his fingers.

'Time we went back to the hotel,' Joe decreed, a little breathlessly.

Her room was sumptuous. The huge bed was covered with green velvet, and there were gold and green cushions strewn about on several antique chairs. The wooden furniture was almost sculpted, and it shone with polish.

The green and golden walls had been decorated with works of art to reflect Venice back to the lucky occupant. There was a statue of a winged lion with his foot on a great book. The golden stallions of St Mark's, of course. In a print of a six-teenth-century oil painting, two bored courtesans played a desultory game with their pet dogs while they waited for night and company. Their elaborately fronded and braided hair amused Alex. Perhaps they had the same problem with curls as she did.

She wandered around exploring, and stopped still in front of a little picture that was not on the walls, but on a small, golden easel on the bureau.

It was later than the other things, perhaps eighteenth cen-tury, she thought. But it was not the masked figures in the painting that attracted Alex's attention. She picked up the pic-ture and turned it over. On the back, a neat line of black type told her it was the *True Portrait of the Elephant brought to Venice in the year 1774 by Pietro Longhi.*

So Joe had found a way to indulge her, after all, thought Alex. This time, she did not wince. She touched a gentle fin-ger to the pictured elephant.

When Joe arrived, she would tell him that she loved him, she thought, suddenly immensely calm.

She had been uncovering the feeling in herself all day. Now it was time to tell the man she loved.

She left the bathroom door open when she took her bath. She did not want to miss his knock.

But he did not come.

For a moment, her confidence faltered. It was not as bad as when she had woken up alone, but it was not good. Then, Alex put on her ruby silk-velvet dress, and a sense of right-ness flooded back. In this gorgeous room, even the shadowed plunge of the neckline did not seem excessive.

If she was going to wear a mask, she did not need much make-up, she thought. But the strange half-faces she had seen in the hotel-display cabinets had all left the mouth and chin free. With a touch of bravado, she painted her mouth crimson.

Then a thought occurred to her. She went back to the print of the bored girls and laughed aloud. All she needed to do was to pile up her hair on the crown of her head. Then she could leave the rest to frizz around her face, as it did naturally, and she would have their hairstyle exactly! She laughed and got to work.

So, when Joe eventually arrived, she had her hair all over the place, and her voluptuously painted mouth full of hairpins.

'G'home… g'hin,' she said through them.

He took the pins out of her mouth. The little gesture was extraordinarily intimate. The inner trembling began again.

He can play me like a lute, Alex thought.

She was rueful. But the old terrible fear of being so completely in his power seemed to have gone – replaced, she thought, by curiosity. What *did* a Red-Hot Lover do, after all?

Aloud, she said, 'Thank you.' And closed the door behind him.

He gave her the hairpins. 'Don't let me interrupt.'

She went back to the mirror and finished fixing her hair with swift efficiency. He sat astride one of the delicate chairs, watching her with deep appreciation.

He was wearing narrow black trousers and a velvet smoking jacket the colour of old burgundy.

'We nearly match,' said Alex, putting her ruby sleeve against his coat.

'Wrong.' He continued to sit astride the chair, looking up at her, his eyes full of laughter and something else she could not quite make out. 'We're a perfect match.'

She made it out. Determination. Well, that could be interesting too.

She said, at random, 'What do you think red-hot lovers do?'

It threw him, as it was supposed to. She enjoyed seeing him disconcerted for a change.

'What brought that up? Which "red-hot lovers"?'

'Oh, it was just Julie.' Alex turned back to the mirror to repair her lipstick, afterwards throwing it over her shoulder naughtily. 'She told me to give her regard to The Red Hot Lover.'

Joe made a shattered sound.

'I just wondered what the qualifications were,' finished Alex airily.

Joe got up slowly. It was not quite menacing. Not *quite*.

'Oh, something along the lines of taking a woman's clothes off between kisses,' he drawled. 'Slowly, of course.'

It was Alex's turn to shiver. 'Of course,' she said in a strangled voice.

'Just as a start.'

'Oh, quite.'

'And then he'd go on to…'

'Right,' she said loudly. 'I'm ready. Shall we go?'

He eyed her up, measuringly. 'You're going to have to finish what you start, you know.'

'I know but – there's a carnival ball to go to, isn't there?' Alex said, flustered.

'Only if you promise you won't run out on me again.' And he was not teasing any more.

There was a tiny silence. Then she nodded. 'I won't run out,' she promised in a low voice.

Joe gave a great sigh. 'Then let's go.'

He held out a mask and a thin fold of silk, which turned out to be a voluminous masquerade cloak, light as thistledown.

'Thank you,' said Alex, leaning into him briefly, as shy as a teenager.

He looked down at her. Beside her, he seemed immensely tall. He said, 'You're welcome.'

And as they were closing the door behind them, he added with great deliberation, 'My love.'

Alex floated into the lift, the lobby, the gondola and, eventually, the ball, as if she was walking on air.

Joe was a possessive escort. He did not let her dance with anyone else. He barely let waiters offer her food and drink. He fed her morsels he had selected, instead. He let her do no more than taste a glass of wine before taking it from her so he could kiss her again.

They danced, copying the steps from their neighbours or improvising wildly. They did stamping country dances, strange, stately, eighteenth-century dances, an uneven waltz, a polka, crazy Latin rhythms. Alex had never done anything like this in her life.

Behind his mask, Joe's eyes glinted, laughing a challenge at her. Behind her own mask, she laughed back. And every time the music brought them together, she felt his hands on her down to her bones.

Eventually, she said in a ragged under-voice, 'I can't take this any more. Take me home. *I need you.*'

His hands were suddenly fierce.

He said roughly, 'I know. Wait here. I'll tell Tom we're going.'

Alex went and leaned against the wall, looking out over the canal. The lights dazzled her, and the blackness outside was mysteriously alluring. It would be heaven to walk through the torch-lit streets with Joe. Heaven and an agony of delayed delight.

She could feel her whole body yield to the prospect.

Turning to look back across the crowded ballroom, she caught sight of Joe… Joe, her love. Without a moment's thought, she swiftly gathered up her skirts and pelted towards her future.

The crowd parted without resistance. She arrived in front of

Joe, laughing and breathless. Behind his mask, his eyes gleamed.

'Hey babe! Tired of dancing, and fancy going for the fifty-metre dash instead?'

Alex took his arm and put it round her waist. 'Only to you.'

His eyes darkened. 'On our way!' he said huskily.

He dropped the silk cloak across her shoulders, and then his arm went around her as if he would never let her go again.

Locked arm in arm, they walked slowly down the steep, crimson-carpeted stairs. The great door to the quay was open. Beyond it, they could see the light from the flambeaux beating in the wind and, beyond the light, the mercurial shift of black water. For a moment, it looked as if they were pacing straight into the unknown. Alex drew closer to him.

Joe looked down at her. 'Scared?'

She hesitated. 'A little,' her instincts said.

He surprised her. 'Yeah. So am I.'

'You? But you're not afraid of anything!'

'Ah, but "Anyone in their right mind approaches a new experience with caution",' he teased.

She groaned. 'What a pompous prat I was. Did you *have* to remember that?'

Joe was unexpectedly serious. 'I remember everything you've ever said to me.'

That silenced her till they reached the doors. Two flunkeys in eighteenth-century costumes and powdered wigs bowed them out. One of them gave Alex a little bag of carnival favours. Joe took it from her and put it in his pocket, as if he had been carrying her stuff all his life.

On the quay the night breeze had a chill in it. Alex's cloak billowed as she shivered. 'I haven't got enough clothes on.'

He handed her into the gondola. 'There's a school of thought that would not agree with that,' he murmured.

And took her in his arms.

The gondolier was not surprised. It was Alex who was surprised. Even now, even knowing she was going home to make love to Joe, she was disconcerted.

'I'm sorry,' she said. 'I suppose I'm not really comfortable with public passion.'

'That's OK,' said Joe easily. 'As long as you know it's passion, I can wait. But let me keep you warm, at least.'

She lay against him, cradled in his arms, looking at the stars. The Grand Canal was crowded, alive with music and laughter and torchlight. But they were in their own little cocoon of magic.

He brushed her fringe of tiny curls away from his mouth and said in her ear, 'So, what are you comfortable with? I haven't done very well, so far. I thought you were going to kill me over those damned marmalade sandwiches.'

She smiled in the darkness. 'Well, you shouldn't have been such a clever clogs. Nobody likes to be wooed to a pre-set programme.'

'At least you knew you were being wooed. I wasn't at all sure about that at the time.'

'I did when I calmed down.' She shifted a little, to look up at him. 'I gave you a bad time, I know. I'm sorry. It wasn't fair.'

'I know it wasn't,' he said cordially. 'That's what gave me hope.'

'*What?*'

'Think about it,' he advised, a laugh in his voice. 'My fair-minded Alex, being *unreasonable*…? You kept making allowances for everybody. You could even see bloody Rupert's point of view. But I only had to make half a mistake, and you flew off the handle. When I stopped swearing, I realised that was a good sign. Losing your cool at last.'

Alex was not sure she liked this aspect of her behaviour.

He kissed her neck, in the tender place just under her ear. She gave a shaky sigh and swayed sideways, offering her throat, trembling.

'You did lose your cool, my darling,' he whispered. 'But not half as much as you are going to tonight.'

Alex was melting. But she could still think. Just.

'So I get to see what a red-hot lover does, after all!' she teased.

The gondola had reached the hotel. Joe handed her out onto the landing stage, paid the gondolier and led her into the golden bustle of the lobby. It was not until they were in her room that he answered her.

'I'm willing to go for the red-hot lover medal,' he told her, laughing, but deeply serious under it. 'And I'll take every single stitch off you, any way you want.'

Alex went very still.

Joe touched her mouth. Behind his own mask, his eyes were tender, and very, very honest.

Alex waited, trembling.

'But... you have to take your mask off yourself.'

She saw he meant it. She even knew why. But it was one of the hardest things she had ever done, untying the mask while he stood so close, watching... watching...

She let it fall. In her nerveless fingers, it weighed nothing. But without it, she felt naked.

Joe took the scrap of papier-mâche away from her. For a moment, he held it against his lips, inhaling. With a little shock, Alex realised that it must still be warm from her face. She gasped, feeling hot suddenly.

That was when he wrenched off his own mask. Without looking, he sent the things spinning to the farthest corner of the room. And they were naked before each other at last.

Alex woke. Her hand was still held in a strong clasp. A possessive arm held her against all the warmth she had ever dreamed of.

Feeling her wake, Joe shifted, raising himself on one elbow to look down at her in the shadows.

'There's just one thing,' he said.

'Mmm?'

Languid with love, Alex burrowed against him. How good his skin smelt.

Joe gave a sensuous laugh. 'You're gorgeous,' he said, momentarily distracted. Then he tipped her chin so she had to look at him. 'But if you want any more – you've got to marry me.'

Alex did not have to think. 'It's a deal,' she said.

'Convinced at last?' Joe teased. 'So I really made it into the red-hot-lover class?'

Alex's blood was stirring. She moved deliberately, hearing with delight his jagged intake of breath.

'You'd better believe it,' she said, closing in. 'Because they don't come any hotter.'

Light. A crowd. A peal of nearby bells.

The light was sunshine. The peal came from a church tower. She was standing in front of it.

Everyone was looking. Alex knew it, and did not care. Joe was besides her, holding her. She could feel his body, its strength and heat. It was familiar now.

'I've found you,' she said, turning to him.

But she could not see him. There was a white mist between them. The bells became foghorns and the cry of gulls. The mist was a swirling lagoon fog.

She was alone again. The sunshine was a fantasy. Joe was a fantasy.

She put out a hand, suddenly fearful.

Another hand took hold of hers.

The mist fell. It was not fog. It was a wedding veil. It was billowing up in the wind. And Joe was wrestling it down, laughing. Laughing straight into her eyes as his hand drew her close...safe for evermore.

We're sure you've enjoyed this month's selection from Heartline. We can offer you even more exciting stories by our talented authors over the coming months. Heartline will be featuring books set in the ever popular and glamorous world of TV - novels with a dash of mystery - a romance featuring two dishy doctors – and just some of the authors we shall be showcasing are Margaret Callaghan, Angela Drake and Kathryn Grant.

If you've enjoyed these books why not tell all your friends and relatives that they, too, can Start a New Romance with Heartline Books today, by applying for their own, **ABSOLUTELY FREE**, copy of Natalie Fox's LOVE IS FOREVER. To obtain their free book, they can:

- visit our website @www.heartlinebooks.com
- *or* telephone the Heartline Hotline on 0845 6000504
- *or* enter their details on the form overleaf, tear off the whole page, and send it to:
  Heartline Books, PO Box 400, Swindon SN2 6EJ

And, like you, they can discover the joys of belonging to Heartline Books Direct™ including:

- ♥ A wide range of quality romantic fiction delivered to their door each month
- ♥ Celebrity interviews
- ♥ A monthly newsletter packed with special offers and competitions
- ♥ Author features
- ♥ A bright, fresh new website created just for our readers

Please send me my free copy of _Love is Forever_:

Name (IN BLOCK CAPITALS)

_____

Address (IN BLOCK CAPITALS)

_____

_____

_____

_____ Postcode _____

If you do not wish to receive selected offers
from other companies, please tick the box ☐

Heartline Books...

Romance at its best ™